W9-BZV-949

WINNERS
AND LOSERS

WINNERS AND LOSERS

STEPHEN HOFFIUS

SIMON & SCHUSTER BOOKS FOR YOUNG READERS
Published by Simon & Schuster
New York   London   Toronto   Sydney   Tokyo   Singapore

SIMON & SCHUSTER BOOKS FOR YOUNG READERS
Simon & Schuster Building, Rockefeller Center
1230 Avenue of the Americas, New York, New York 10020
Copyright © 1993 by Stephen Hoffius
All rights reserved including the right of reproduction
in whole or in part in any form.
SIMON & SCHUSTER BOOKS FOR YOUNG READERS
is a trademark of Simon & Schuster.
Designed by Vicki Kalajian.
The text for this book was set in 11 point ITC Century Book.
Manufactured in the United States of America

10   9   8   7   6   5   4   3   2   1

Library of Congress Cataloging-in-Publication Data
Hoffius, Stephen. Winners and losers / by Stephen Hoffius.
p.   cm.   Summary: When a heart condition threatens to curtail
his friend Daryl's track career, Curt finds himself
taking Daryl's place as lead contender
for the conference championship and as the
new obsession of Daryl's driven father.
[1. Track and field—Fiction.   2. Winning and losing—Fiction.
3. Friendship—Fiction.   4. Fathers and sons—Fiction.]
I. Title.   PZ7.H6744Wi   1993   [Fic]—dc20
92–42394   CIP   ISBN: 0–671–79194–X

For
Susan

WINNERS
AND LOSERS

CHAPTER ONE

Daryl Wagner was rounding the last turn of the half-mile, the finish line in sight, when his heart stopped beating.

It was the first track meet of the year, and all of us at Hasely High were psyched. We knew Georgetown would give us our toughest challenge. Coach Kirby had been talking about it for weeks. Daryl's dad, who was unofficial coach for Daryl and me, had been talking about it even longer. Daryl and Georgetown's Will Stewart were expected to be the two fastest half-milers in the conference.

Daryl and Stewart had rocketed away at the gun, lots faster than me. I had a hard time just keeping up with the guy in third, a skinny, redheaded kid from Georgetown. He slowed down at all the turns, so I caught him there, but on the straightaways he pulled away from me.

At the end of the first lap, the redhead had been just a stride in front. I kept my eyes on his shoulders and neck, watching them turn pink, then red. I repeated to myself, "No pain, no gain, no pain, no gain," the way Daryl's father had taught us, until there was nothing else in my mind. Daryl and Will Stewart were already into the next turn.

Daryl's father was standing at the line, leaning out over the track. Two stopwatches hung from his neck, one in each hand. The one in his right hand was for Daryl, the other for me. As I went past him, starting the second and last lap, he called out my time: "61, 62." It was slower than I had wanted to run. Mr. Wagner's voice was flat, as if I'd let him down.

Years ago, he had run the half-mile in high school and college. If Daryl worked hard, Mr. Wagner said, he could win the regular season title. Maybe he could even break what Mr. Wagner called the Family Record—1 minute and 57.6 seconds. That was Mr. Wagner's best time in college. The tracks and shoes are better now than they were then, at least that's what he kept telling us, so maybe Daryl could run that as a high school freshman. And this year would be his only chance. Next year our whole conference would change to metric distances. We'd run 800 meters, not 880 yards. Mr. Wagner said I might be able to place third in the conference, behind Daryl and Will Stewart.

But I wasn't even third in this race. The redhead never got far ahead of me, but I couldn't pass him either. As I hit the last turns of the second lap, I saw that we were both catching Daryl. By then, Will Stewart was almost at the finish line and Daryl was way behind. He didn't even look back as the redhead and I came up. His feet splayed out to the right and to the left and his arms flapped wildly. I thought, Uh-oh, his old man's gonna scream. Mr. Wagner had put a lot of time into our training. The way Daryl was staggering broke every rule we'd been taught.

The redhead went around Daryl and I was a step behind. I glanced back to see what the matter was, but Daryl's head was down so I couldn't see his face. As I headed down the final stretch, I could see Mr. Wagner standing by the finish, looking toward us. He always wore those mirrored sunglasses as if he were an airline pilot. He turned his head from me to Daryl, who was still behind me. The only sounds I could hear were my own gasping and my cleats digging into the track. I took third.

I ran through the finish, the way Mr. Wagner had taught us, not slowing down just before the line the way some guys do. A lot of races get lost right there. I walked along with my hands on my hips and my head down. Jim Ryun walked like that after he set the world's record in the mile.

But when I turned around, no one even congratulated me. Everyone was running back to where Daryl lay on the track. Coach Kirby was racing across the field toward the fire station.

I turned back, wondering what had happened. After a race, you should always walk it off. If you lie down, you'll get a sideache. Daryl knew that. I was a little mad. Even when I beat him, I thought, he still gets all the attention.

By the time I reached the crowd, I could hear the shriek of an ambulance in the distance. Jaryld Whitson's father, who was a doctor, was on his knees beside Daryl, pushing on his chest. Cathy Daniels, Daryl's girlfriend, was with a bunch of her friends, hiding her face.

Someone said that Daryl's heart had stopped. He was dead. *Dead?* How could that be? Daryl's an athlete, he runs track and is on the football team. He'd been training all year, even running the streets in the winter before the snowplows could scrape down to the concrete. He was in great shape. But there he lay, not moving, while a doctor pounded his chest with all his strength. Dead? My best friend? I pushed through the crowd to get to him.

I should have stopped to help him instead of running past. I knew that as soon as I saw him there. I had cared more about finishing than about helping my best friend.

Daryl and I lived a block apart. When I wasn't at his

house, he was almost always at mine. We did every-thing together, even when he made the varsity football team as a freshman and I was just second-string junior varsity. He was smarter than me and a better athlete, but we were still best friends. His father called me his second son.

Finally, I elbowed my way through the crowd to where Daryl still lay on his back, limp. He looked like he really could be dead. His eyes were closed. His face and arms were pale, and he only moved when Dr. Whit-son pushed on his chest. I heard people whispering, "Is he dead? Is he dead?"

"No," I shouted. "He's fine!" My face felt hot and it was hard to breathe. He couldn't be dead, I thought. Not Daryl.

Dr. Whitson wiggled his finger around Daryl's tongue, leaned down, and put his mouth over Daryl's as if they were kissing. Then he straightened up and gasped, and did it again.

Mr. Wagner knelt down beside Daryl, the two stop-watches dangling from his neck. The hands of one were still spinning, as if the race were not over yet. He stared down at Daryl and didn't answer when people asked him questions. But no one said much.

Then an ambulance rushed screaming through the tennis courts. Three men in white uniforms jumped out and ran up to Daryl.

"I've got a pulse," Dr. Whitson yelled to them. So he

hadn't died! I closed my eyes and let my head drop back. He was alive! I took a deep breath.

They lifted Daryl onto a stretcher and carried him to the ambulance. A man there shouted, "Give him room, people. He needs air." One of Daryl's arms hung down loose. He looked like a gunfighter in a movie lying across the back of a horse. The door swung open. A woman was sitting inside, waiting for him.

Daryl's father started for the ambulance. Then he saw me. His jaw was set, his face tight. He looked like those actors in war movies, the ones who think the future of the world depends on them. His sunglasses were in his hand. He laid his hand on my shoulder and looked me in the eye. The way he looked, I wondered at first if he was angry. "He'll be all right, Curt." I just nodded.

"You looked good in that race." Mr. Wagner's voice was steady and low, like this was talk for men only. "You could have gone out stronger. But you got third?" I nodded again.

"Good job." He squeezed my shoulder, looking at me in a new way, as if he hadn't seen me a thousand times before. Then Mr. Wagner climbed in the open ambulance door.

The doctors were bent over Daryl, who was covered with a sheet. The door closed and the ambulance sped off through the tennis courts. The red light on top was spinning around and the shriek of the siren filled the track.

Someone grabbed my arm and pulled me to the infield. I heard one of the coaches say they were going to continue the meet. Daryl was alive, and it was time for the 220.

CHAPTER TWO

I never did see Daryl that night. By the time I got to the hospital, about ten o'clock, they said he was asleep and couldn't have any visitors. But I don't think he had gone to sleep before eleven or twelve since he was a kid. And I wasn't a *visitor*. I was his best friend!

The story about Daryl was on the television news that night. One station even had a film of the race. My parents and I watched the eleven o'clock news, lying on the big bed in their room.

On the news, Daryl looked great until the last turn, pounding his arms back and forth, stretching out his legs, bent at the waist just a little. Just like we'd been taught. Then he stumbled at the last turn and slowed down. When he did, my mom covered her eyes and said "Oh, God!" My dad reached past me to hold her hand.

Around that turn, Daryl's legs still moved but you could see they didn't have any power. Finally, he just collapsed on his left side, crumpling onto his elbow, hip, and shoulder. When he hit the track I flinched. Then, on the TV, you could see me pass him, mostly just my legs and shoes. My dad said Daryl must have been running even after his heart had stopped, like those chickens who run around after their heads have been cut off. They called it a cardiac arrest and said he ran faster than his heart could stand. But how can a person go that fast? It didn't seem possible.

I said to my parents, "Cardiac arrest? That sounds like his heart was busted for speeding."

My mom shook her head. "It's a heart attack, honey. His heart stopped beating." On the TV they showed Dr. Whitson bending over Daryl, pushing on his chest.

"I thought only old people got heart attacks."

"Usually that's true," explained my mom, who had turned to look right at me. "But young people sometimes—not very often, but sometimes—have them because they were born with something wrong with their hearts. And middle-aged people get heart attacks for lots of reasons. Like ..." She paused and looked over at my dad. "Like when they're too heavy and make their hearts work too hard."

She kept her eyes on him. I did too. Finally he noticed and jerked his head in surprise. "Hey! Why you looking at me?" He didn't get it. My dad's stomach hangs way over his belt because he never does anything special for exercise. Mom bugs him about it, and I do too, but he ignores us both. "Hey, listen to this," he said, pointing to a story on the TV about baseball. He didn't want to talk about heart attacks.

I didn't either. But I couldn't help wondering about Daryl. He was born with a bad heart? This super jock had had a bad heart all these years? And then my eyes opened wide when the thought hit me: was mine okay, or could the same thing happen to me?

For the first time in years I just wanted to stay there in my parents' king-size bed, watching the tube, watching junk, anything. I didn't want to leave that warm, safe place. I stayed between them, looking at the set until I fell asleep. The next morning I woke up in my own bed. I had no memory of what we'd seen after the sports.

Usually in the morning, Daryl came over to our house and we walked to school together. Even after he ate breakfast at his house, he still would eat a bagel or some bacon and toast while he waited for me. Mom always made more than we needed, knowing he was coming. She cooked for him the day after the accident too, four pancakes more than we could eat. They lay on a plate by the stove, getting cold and the butter congealing.

"How do you feel, Curt?" my mom asked.

"I'm okay," I said, "just sleepy." I had dreamed about Daryl falling onto the track, landing on his shoulder and rolling. He kept doing it—stumbling, falling, and rolling—and I woke up when I ran past him. I never looked down at him, but I knew he was there and I kept going.

"You better get to school, Curt," Mom said finally, when I either had to leave or be late. The walk seemed to take forever. And then when I got there and walked through the door, I didn't know what to do. I always hung out with Daryl and he wasn't there.

But his girlfriend Cathy was, standing near the lockers, and she had a big crowd around her. I could hear that Cathy had made up a more exciting story than I ever could. She said she had known that something was wrong, even before the meet. "Daryl seemed tense all day," she said. "I could see it in his eyes."

Well, heck yes, he was tense! It was the first meet of the year! I turned away when I heard that, but she saw me and left her friends to come over.

Cathy and I have never gotten along well. I know she's beautiful, with black hair cut almost as short as a boy's and a knock-out smile like a movie star's or a model's. But sometimes she's pretty stuck-up too. I've double-dated with her and Daryl and I always got the feeling that she didn't want me around. I heard her ask

11

once, "Oh, do we have to go with Curtis again?" Not that they were going to do anything hot, Daryl would have told me that, but I guess just because I wasn't as important as they were. They were both great-looking, they got A's whether or not they studied, and they were the best athletes in the class. I had played tennis with Cathy once and only won two games. That was the last time I did that!

"Curtis," she called as she ran toward me. The people who had been around her surrounded both of us. My face was probably bright red. It always is when people look at me. "Oh, Curtis," she sobbed, and then buried her head in my shoulder. She was wearing perfume, even at school, and with Daryl in the hospital! She pressed against me, her head turned sideways so I could feel her tears on my neck. I put my arms around her. What was I supposed to do? At first I figured she was just putting on a show so everyone would sympathize with her. It was embarrassing, with everybody watching, but she did feel good to hold. I was surprised how strong her back muscles were, stronger than you'd think for a tennis player. After a while, I didn't even mind the perfume.

"Mrs. Wagner called me last night," she said, looking up at me. "She said Daryl was doing all right." Cathy's eyes were red. "He's got to stay in the hospital a couple of days, but he'll be able to come back to school next week. She asked me to take his books to the hospital."

I laughed at that. "Jeez, even when you almost die, they won't let you forget your homework." Cathy glared at me, as if I wasn't supposed to mention the heart attack.

"Mrs. Wagner said he asked for you." That's what she said. He had asked for me. But Mrs. Wagner never called. She knows my number better than she knows Cathy's. It's on the wall in the kitchen, right next to the phone. I saw Daryl write it. But for some reason she called his girlfriend instead of me.

"Curtis, do you understand it?" Most of the people had left but Cathy was still standing there, looking up at me like she wasn't just acting upset. "How could he have a heart attack? How?" I told her what my mom had said, that he must have been born with a heart problem.

"I know," she said even before I finished. "Mrs. Wagner said something about the walls of the chambers of his heart being too thick."

I pursed my lips. This was getting ridiculous! Cathy was being told all this news as if she were a member of the family, and I was being ignored! I tried to remember from biology class the shape of a heart. The walls of what chambers were too thick?

"I'm going to the hospital after school," she said. "Visiting hours are four to six. Do you want a ride?"

I shook my head. "Not then," I explained. "I'll go after practice."

"Practice?" she shouted. "You're going back to track? After it almost killed Daryl?" She was getting hysterical.

"You know he's not exactly dead," I said, lowering my voice, trying to keep from being heard by every kid in the school.

"Not yet," she said even louder. "He was lucky." She jerked her head around as if she were looking for someone who would agree with her. People started to come back. "But who *will* be the first one to die, the way they push guys in sports? You? Danny?" Danny was her brother, a year older than us. The only way Danny would ever move faster than his heart could take would be if someone left a big steak at the finish line. That kid looked like he lived for food and nothing else.

All around us people were murmuring, "Yeah." "That's right." "And football's even worse."

"You can't blame track for what happened to Daryl," I said. She of all people—another athlete—should have known that!

"No?" Cathy turned on me abruptly. Her face was wet, with red blotches all over it. "Then whose fault is it?"

My head felt like it was spinning. I didn't know all the

answers. I didn't understand how Daryl could have collapsed. "It was nobody's fault." I wanted to sound casual, as if it all made sense. "It just happened." That seemed pretty cold, when a guy is lying in the hospital with a heart that stopped. But all I knew was that before the meet he was as psyched to run well as anyone could be, he was in great shape, he'd trained hard. And for some reason he couldn't even finish the race.

"It just happened," repeated Cathy, a strained smile on her lips. "Sure."

That afternoon, Coach Kirby called the team together near the high-jump pit. He told us that Daryl was okay. He said a cardiac arrest was a fluke, one in a million, and we shouldn't worry about it happening to us. He repeated the story about the thickness of the chamber walls in Daryl's heart, and said he had an irregular heartbeat. We talked about other weird sports accidents that guys knew about. Everybody remembered people who smashed their knees on their first day in pro football, things like that. A lot of the guys touched their chests, as if they were making sure their own hearts were still beating.

Coach said we had beaten Georgetown by only three points. Not much. And since Daryl wouldn't be able to run anymore, that meant everyone else would have to improve a lot before the championship. I knew that meant me. I was the number one half-miler now.

Coach had us run distances that day, figure eights that went up around the football field and then down the hill and around the track. Each one was about six-tenths of a mile. The half-milers had to run ten of them. That was okay with me. When I got going I could run distances forever. "Just go steady," said Coach. "Don't feel you have to push yourselves today."

He took me aside for a special talk. All the guys were watching, wondering what he would say. "So how do you feel about running now?" he asked.

I looked up in surprise. "Are you kicking me off the team?"

He shook his head. "No, I'm just asking. I'd expect you to feel pretty shook up after yesterday's experience. Don't you?" It sounded like a challenge.

"Well, yeah, but I'm still ready to run."

"I think Daryl would want you to."

No, he wouldn't, I thought. Daryl wouldn't be thinking about me at all. He's probably cussing a lot. He's wishing that *he* were running. And maybe he's apologizing to his dad, who must be totally bummed. This ruins Mr. Wagner's season as much as it does Daryl's.

"Go on back with the other half-milers," said Coach. "Take them through the figure eights but don't run more than feels comfortable." The guys were waiting for me.

We all took off, running the first lap fast but then slowing down to a pace we could maintain for six miles. My hair slapped against the back of my neck and blew back from my forehead. I had a good lead and it felt fast.

When I first went out for track two years ago, I chose the half, 880 yards, because it's not boring like the longer races, and you don't have to be the fastest guy around like in the sprints. You need strategy for the half, but it's over in just a little more than two minutes. Also, except for Daryl, the rest of the half-milers weren't that good.

We came down the hill and then around the turn where Daryl had collapsed. For some reason, I expected to see something there. Blood, maybe, though I knew he hadn't bled. Or a silhouette of his body, like they found in Hiroshima after the bomb was dropped. There was nothing, just the lane lines stretching into the distance.

The last lap I kicked it in. I was breathing deeply and could feel my legs stretching out, gobbling up the distances. I love to run, like nothing else I do. This workout felt super, and different from all the others. Usually I ran side by side with Daryl until the last lap or two when he would leave me behind. Then I had to struggle to stay close. After talking with Cathy that day, when she said that track had almost killed him, I wondered if

I would ever want to run again, if it would just be like the nightmare I'd had. But this felt great. I kept pouring it on, stretching out my stride, picking up the pace.

After I finished, I looked back. The other guys were coming down the hill. I had beaten them by more than two hundred yards. Then I heard a yell.

"Hey, Mick Jagger!" It was Daryl's dad. He was coming across the field in his pin-striped businessman's suit, aviator shades, and crewcut. He had always worn a crewcut, whether everyone else did or he was the only one.

"Hey, Jagger! Can't you see me through that wig?" Everyone on the track—maybe everyone in the city—could hear him. They turned to look at us.

"Hi, Mr. Wagner. How's Daryl?"

"He's doing fine." Mr. Wagner clasped his hands behind his back, very military, and looked around the track. "He's a little embarrassed about collapsing like that, but his doctors say they can give him some medicine that will make him good as new in no time." Then he stopped gazing all over the track and looked at me. "So how was the workout?" In his glasses, I could see my face stretch back, like I was all nose and cheeks. I tried to look away.

"Not bad," I said. "It wasn't too hard."

He shook his head and scowled. "Kirby's never going to get you in shape." He always thought Coach should push us more, as if we were all going to the Olympics.

"Listen, Curt." He put his arm on my shoulder. I was dripping wet. His suit coat would get soaked but he didn't seem to care. "This is a big week for you."

I looked at him, puzzled. "Why?"

He stepped back as if I were an idiot. He was about my height and weighed just a little bit more. He played racquetball almost every noon, was champion at the downtown athletic club, and had trophies all over his house. "You're number one now," he said. "Just like you've always wanted."

"I haven't always wanted that," I said, but of course I'd thought about it. It just seemed creepy to mention it.

"Now it's your turn to shine," he said. "Daryl could have won the conference before this happened. Now you can."

I stopped. To see Mr. Wagner, I had to look right into the sun. I held my hand over my eyes but then he looked fuzzy, with no facial features. He was just a voice, insistent, constant. I looked away. "I can't win the conference," I told him. "Will Stewart's got almost five seconds on me."

"You can break two minutes," he said. I almost laughed at him. My best time was 2:06, from the day before.

"Well, maybe," I said, and started for the locker room. He held my arm, and turned me back toward the track.

"I'm serious, Curt. You'll have to work. Kirby lets you

dog it way too much in practice. It showed in the meet yesterday. You should have had second place. But if you push yourself, you can win. Don't you *want* to win the conference?"

" 'Course I do." Who wouldn't, I thought, but I'd never been first in anything. "I'll think about it, anyway," I said.

"You'll have to do more than that." Mr. Wagner hadn't let go of my arm. "Will Stewart isn't just thinking about it, and he's your main competition."

"I know that," I said. "But I'm going to go see Daryl now." I pictured him in the hospital with Cathy Daniels sniffling in the chair next to him. I wanted to rescue him from that mushiness that I knew he hated.

"You've missed most of the four-to-six already," he said. "Visiting hours open up again between seven and nine. You can go then." Most of the guys had already left for the locker room. Robbie Bester and some others were lying in the pole-vault pit, probably talking about girls. Robbie came to practice every day but he never applied himself. That's what Coach said. He was barely on the team.

"Come over here," Mr. Wagner said. Coach Kirby had left out a starting block. We walked over to it. Nobody used a block for the half-mile. That was for sprinters. "Let's work on that slow-motion start of yours," he said. He dropped the block just behind the starting line and kicked the stakes into the holes in the track. It seemed crazy. A block for the half was overkill.

But then I thought, You're number one. If you want to stay there, it'll mean work. "No pain, no gain." Mr. Wagner patted my butt. I hadn't meant to say that out loud.

"You got it, Curt," he said. "No pain, no gain. And you can get a haircut tomorrow."

I groaned.

CHAPTER THREE

Cathy could take Daryl his schoolbooks. He didn't want them anyway. I stopped at Remes Drug Store on my way to the hospital that night and bought copies of *Mad* and *Sports Illustrated*. I couldn't see him sitting in bed all day reading *Silas Marner*.

The hospital was a big brick building about two miles from my house. I'd passed it plenty of times, had watched ambulances rush to it, but I'd never been in it before. It seemed like someplace evil, where bad things happened. Like a jail. If it had been anyone but Daryl, I wouldn't have gone. The lobby had been decorated with abstract art and bright colors—streaks and smears—but it still seemed bleak. It smelled like something sick. I rode up to the third floor with a man and a woman who looked like they hadn't been in the sun in years. They wouldn't raise their eyes from the floor. I wondered how Daryl could possibly recover in a place like that.

He had a room to himself. As I walked in, he was sitting up in bed, watching TV. It was a black-and-white sitcom from about twenty years ago, something stupid that he would never have watched if he'd had anything else to do. There were about half a dozen bouquets of flowers around the room. He looked pretty good, except he was wearing funny blue and yellow pajamas and had on a dinky plastic bracelet.

Daryl has this huge chest from lifting weights that his dad bought him last year. At first, Daryl didn't want to mess around with them—it was just another order from his old man—but then he got into it. He even got a little crazy about them. Every night he would go down to his basement and work out. He'd press them, clean and jerk, do some curls, the whole bit. Sometimes I'd spot for him. He'd spot for me too, but I didn't do it nearly as much as he did. He liked to wear short-sleeved shirts with the sleeves rolled back to his shoulders so you could see the muscles rippling down his arms. When he put on a track jersey with straps like old men's undershirts, all the girls stared.

"Hey, it's about time you got here," he said when he saw me. He clicked off the TV with the remote. "Where've you been?"

"Been busy with this nurse down the hall," I told him, trying not to smile.

"Yeah, I know which one you mean," he said. "The one with the mustache. She brought me dinner."

"Dinner?" I made a shocked expression. "She said that was a sample from one of the other patients."

"Hmmm," he said, licking his lips. "Tasted good, though."

I couldn't help but smile at that. I don't know what I would have done if *I'd* almost died the day before, but there's no way I would've been all casual like that, making jokes.

"I brought you some literature," I said, and tossed him the magazines.

He broke into a big smile. "That's more like it! Look what Cathy brought." He pointed to a pile of school-books about a foot high on the bedside table. They didn't look like they'd been touched yet. On top was a new pair of weights, the kind you snap around your wrists or ankles with Velcro.

"Where'd you get those?" I asked.

He shrugged. "Where do you think? My old man." We both laughed. It was just like Mr. Wagner not to let him rest even a day. "But the doctors won't let me wear them until tomorrow."

"Is that all? I figured you wouldn't be able to do anything for a month or two." I sat on the edge of the bed. He shoved over to give me room, then leaned back.

"Nah, it's not that big a deal now. I'm pretty much recovered already. I tried to tell them I couldn't mow the lawn anymore, but that didn't fly."

I shook my head. "How can you collapse one day and be recovered the next? Don't they have to do surgery?"

"No, nothing like that." He dropped his voice like he didn't want to talk about it, but he continued. "There's a name for this—asymmetric hyper-something. I don't know what it is." He hurried on as if he could tell how confused it sounded. "But they've got some pills for me—beta blockers—that will take care of it. As long as I take the pills I'm fine."

Even as he said he was fine, I thought about seeing him fall on television. "Hey," I said, and now my voice was soft too. "I'm sorry I didn't stop. I didn't realize what was happening."

He scowled as if I were crazy. "Why would you stop? What could you do?"

"I don't know, but—"

"My old man said you took third?"

"Yeah, but only because of you."

"Coach is going to expect it regularly from now on."

"He already does."

All the time we were talking, Daryl was adjusting his bed. The head and feet went up and down, and the whole thing rose up toward the ceiling. I took the control from his hand, eager to stop talking about the race, and tried other positions. Once I got the feet so high I slid down toward Daryl. I was just putting it back when Daryl said, "You know, this has possibilities. Man, I'd love to get Cathy on this thing." Just then his mom peeked around the door and walked in. I don't think she heard him. I hope not. She doesn't have much of a sense of humor.

She's a little woman, shorter than either of us, but kind of pretty for a mother. Her hair is short and black. It curls so tight around her ears it looks like plastic. Everyone else's hair gets messed up sometimes but not Mrs. Wagner's. That day she was even paler than usual. Daryl and his dad were always tanned deep brown all summer but Mrs. Wagner never seemed to leave the house much.

Daryl said his dad didn't want her to work a regular job, but man, could she cook! She could have run her own restaurant if she wanted to. In her hand was a tin box. We both knew right away that it was filled with cookies. She did that kind of thing—cookies, cakes, pies.

"Oh. Hello, Curtis," she said when she saw me. The big smile across her face faded as if she were sorry I was there. That kind of hurt. Usually she was real nice to me. But once I'd heard her yell at Mr. Wagner that he and Daryl and I were all on a team, working against her.

"Would you like a cookie?" she asked, holding out the box toward me.

Daryl leaned forward and shouted, "Hey! Who's the sick man here?"

"All right, Daryl," she said, this big smile across her face. "You can get away with no manners just this once."

She popped the top and steam rose up. The box was filled with huge chocolate-chip oatmeal cookies.

"All ri-i-ight," Daryl shouted, and leaned toward them. He picked up a cookie and took a big bite. A smudge of chocolate chip stuck to his lower lip. Then he dropped the cookie onto the bed and grabbed his chest. He tensed up. His face trembled a little and his eyes bugged out. He made little choking noises and fell back onto the pillow.

"Oh, my God!" whispered his mother, and she dropped the tin of cookies onto the bed. I grabbed them. I knew what he was doing.

"Mom, Mom," gasped Daryl. He seemed like he needed all his strength just to raise one finger. He motioned for her to approach. When she did, he whispered, "Next . . . time . . ." He stopped and caught his breath.

"Wait, wait a moment, dear," his mother said nervously. "Don't waste your energy." Her head jerked around like she thought she'd find a doctor hidden in the room somewhere if only she looked hard enough. She grabbed the call button and pounded on it. I thought she might break it. "Nurse!" she cried. "Nurse!"

"Next . . . time," Daryl continued, working for each breath, *"bring . . . more . . . cookies."* Then he collapsed back. For a moment, the room was silent as she stared at him, trying to understand what he had said. The only sound was me, eating.

Then, still flat on his back, eyes closed, Daryl found his fallen cookie and placed it in his mouth. When Mrs. Wagner saw that, I thought she would bash him.

A nurse rushed into the room. "Yes?" she asked. "What's the matter?"

Mrs. Wagner's lips were pursed together. "My son," she explained, one word at a time, "has just made a *fool* of me, that's all." She shook her head angrily. "Nothing. It's nothing. I should be used to it by now. I'm sorry to have bothered you."

The nurse nodded to Mrs. Wagner. I thought I saw her left eye close and open quickly. Then she took Daryl's wrist in her hand. She studied her watch, listening intently. "Uh-oh," said the nurse. "This could be serious."

Daryl looked up in surprise. "Hey, I was just kidding," he said. "I feel fine."

The nurse shook her head. "No, you shouldn't eat these anyway," she said. "Too high in cholesterol." She turned to Mrs. Wagner, with this big smile on her face. "What do you think?"

"Absolutely," she said. Mrs. Wagner had a guilty grin,

like she couldn't believe what naughtiness she was doing. "Curtis, do you think you could finish these?"

I took my own pulse and nodded. "Yes, ma'am. My heart feels stronger than ever. No problem here." I reached for the cookie box as Mr. Wagner entered the room.

"Hey, what goes on here?" he asked, looking over the scene. "One boy's sick and gets no life-sustaining sweets? The other's in training, and does? This is backward."

Mrs. Wagner stood up and stepped back, away from Daryl. The nurse looked confused for a moment, then slipped out the door. Mr. Wagner took her place by the bed. He took the tin from me and returned it to Daryl, who pushed it away.

"The two top runners! The one who could have been conference champ and the one who will be." He wagged his finger at me. "*If* he ever stops walking the first hundred yards."

I groaned. We waited for Mr. Wagner to continue. He always had more to say.

"The good news for Daryl is that he can ease off his training. And the good news for Mop-Top Curt," he said, putting his face right up to mine, "is that you can increase yours!" He had made his hands into fists, as if this were a pre-race pep talk.

"Lucky you," muttered Daryl. His mother took his hand.

"And his reward could be the Family Record!"

"What's mine?" asked Daryl from his bed.

His mother put her arm around his neck and leaned close. "Life," she whispered loudly.

Mr. Wagner left me and put his hand out for Daryl to slap. "Not a bad second prize," he said, "don't you think?"

Daryl grinned. "I guess I'll take it," he said as his hand landed on his father's.

CHAPTER FOUR

The next Wednesday, when Daryl came back to school, it was just like before. He came by my house in the morning and finished off a container of yogurt. Then we walked to school. He wanted to know what had been happening while he was gone. He said most of what he knew about the last week at school was what Cathy had told him, and that was just about the girls. So we yakked while we walked. The sun was so warm we didn't need sweaters or coats and we reached school happy and hot.

Then this crowd descended on us. It seemed like everyone wanted to check in with Daryl—"How you doing, man?" "Looking good, you feeling good?"

People gathered around him wherever he went. Girls, of course, watched everything he did. They always had. But now, even some of the seniors came up to talk with him. Daryl was a celebrity, more popular than if he'd just beaten Will Stewart. Anybody else would have acted like a big shot.

Not Daryl.

"How you feeling?" some guy would ask him. "Hungry," he'd say. "Same as always."

"Oh, Daryl, I was so scared," one girl said.

"It was just a way to get out of class," he said. "Hey, did that algebra make any sense to you?"

He didn't just make a joke out of everything, he tried to change the subject, tried to get people to talk about other things. Sometimes, though, it didn't work. "Oh, Daryl," said one girl. "We were so worried about you." At first you could see by his grin that he was looking for a way to make a joke about what she had said, but something in her face, her eyes maybe, caught him, and he just said, "Yeah. Well, thanks, Sandy."

All that week, I worked at practice like never before. I was first in everything—wind sprints, distances, even when we just strided down the infield to loosen up. Then, after practice, Mr. Wagner and I worked on my starts. It took me a while to get used to a block, trying to figure out where to put the foot pieces. Some of the guys thought it was showing off to use it, but Mr. Wagner said I needed it to make up for my slow start.

We were doing quarter-miles at medium speed Thursday when Daryl showed up at practice. He was wearing running shorts, a T-shirt, and an old pair of Nikes. He came into the infield, sat down, and stretched with the team. He put one leg out, then the other. Did the bicycle. Just the basic exercises we'd done since grade school, nothing fancy, but it scared me to see him. I went over to him when we had a break. "You sure you ought to be doing that?" I asked him.

"Don't worry about me," he said. "I'm just staying loose." Around his ankles he wore the new weights his dad had given him. "You look pretty good out there."

I shrugged. "Got a long ways to go."

He shook his head and continued stretching, his back to me. "Better watch out. You're beginning to sound like my old man." I didn't know what that was supposed to mean. Did he expect me to say no to his dad, the first person who thought I could amount to something as a runner? I wondered if maybe, for the first time in his life, Daryl was jealous of me.

When Coach called us together, Daryl went over to the track. We sat in a circle while Coach and his assistants talked about the next day's meet with Grandville, but no one listened. We all watched Daryl, wondering what he would do.

First, he just walked along real slow until the first turn. Then he started to jog. Not fast or anything, probably only a quick walk, but he lifted his knees as if he was serious about it. He took forever to cover the backstretch. Still, he was running. I think everybody's heart started pounding double-time just watching him.

When he came by the high-jump pit where we were sitting, we all stared. That was where he had fallen. But he kept going, still slow, maybe even ten minutes for the quarter-mile. Once he could have run it in fifty-three seconds. He stared straight ahead, a hundred per-cent concentration, as if it were the conference championship or something.

One of the assistant coaches, Mr. Pomeroy, joined him for the last fifty yards. They talked as they moved along but Daryl never turned his head to the right or to the left. He continued as far as the finish line, one full lap, and then stopped. He probably hadn't even raised a sweat, but none of us could relax until he had finished. When he did, we all breathed out at once, and turned back to the group.

Coach went through each event, telling us how he expected us to finish. When he got to the half, he said, "Curtis, you ought to win this one." I nodded and looked away, as if I took that for granted. "Their top half-miler's best time is about 2:08," he added. "You ran 2:06 last week. You should be able to get even lower than that, but you'll have to take the lead fast, hold it through the quarter, and then stretch it out." I kept on nodding, chewing gum, glancing back at Daryl. He was stretching on the hurdles. "Do you hear me?" Coach yelled. He had his hands on his hips and was staring at me, as if I had already let him down.

"Sure." I tried to sound cool. "I'll win it."

When Mr. Wagner arrived, Daryl was already gone. I told him Daryl had been there, and he smiled in that know-it-all way he had. "Once a real athlete gets bit by sports," he said, "he can't ever get away from it. It'll be hard for him, but the doctor said he can exercise again in a few weeks. He'll probably never race again, but he doesn't have to turn into a couch potato. He'll just have to star in the classroom from now on."

Since the Grandville race was the next day, Mr. Wagner and I didn't work out much. Mostly we talked strategy, like how to avoid getting boxed, when to pass, things like that. I took a few starts, exploding from the blocks with my arms churning forward, so I could be in the lead at the first turn. I think it helped. As I took off from the blocks and raced thirty or forty yards down the track, I felt like I could beat anyone.

Later, with every step of the walk home, I went over the next day's race in my mind. Especially the finish. I pictured myself throwing out my chest and breaking the tape. It seemed like I'd seen that a thousand times—other people winning, never me. The tape would stretch back, snap, and flutter to the ground. At least that's how I pictured it. The tape worried me a little. Of course, they don't really hold a piece of masking tape or anything. They use string. But I've tried to break some pieces of string with my hands and couldn't. They dug into my hands like wire. I'd never broken a finish-line string before, and I didn't know what it would feel like.

So far, the best I'd done was third place. That scored one point for the team. A first-place finish would count five points. The guys who did well sometimes boasted to each other about the number of points they'd scored. Now maybe I'd be able to say something too.

When I walked in the door, I saw my dad in the kitchen. Mom was working late. Dad was a pretty good cook, usually pork chops or something easy and a frozen vegetable. He wasn't as good as Mom but a lot better than me. Once I even burned canned soup. "Hi, what's for dinner?" I asked. My dad turned, and smiled a greeting.

When he smiled you could see he had two or three chins. He probably outweighed me by fifty pounds, although he was only a little taller than me. He'd never played any sports and when he stood next to Mr. Wagner or somebody else who was in good shape, the difference was embarrassing. "Hi," he said. "Chicken."

"Oh." I tried to say it casually, but he could tell that I was disappointed.

"What's the matter?" There was a chicken on the counter, almost pale white, and he was slicing through the joints with a long knife. To his side was a pile of legs and wings that he'd already cut.

"Nothing," I said. "That's fine."

He stopped, put down the knife, and rinsed off his

hands. "No, what's the matter?" He'd gotten a piece of white chicken fat on his mustache, but he wiped it off.

"It's nothing," I said. "We've just got a meet tomorrow, that's all."

"Does chicken break training for you?" I don't think he'd ever run in his life. He knew nothing about training. How much would I have to teach him?

"No, it's fine. It's just not high carb, that's all."

"High carb?" He looked like he might laugh.

"Forget it," I said, and started up for my room.

"No, tell me," he said quickly. "What's high carb?"

"Carbohydrates." It was hard to say that without sounding like a teacher. "It's what you're supposed to eat before a meet. Helps you run." Actually, I couldn't remember how it was supposed to help, whether it produced sugar, or built up strength, or what. But I'd read that the night before the Boston Marathon, all the runners pump carbs. Spaghetti and beer are served free to the runners at some bar in town. It's supposed to help them get past Heartbreak Hill.

"Like what kinds of foods?" He leaned back against the counter, his arms crossed on his chest.

Nothing made my dad happier than asking questions. He could ask a million about almost anything. Usually he seemed like he genuinely cared what the answer was, but sometimes I could tell he was just asking questions to make me think, as if he were giving me a test. But I couldn't always tell when he cared and when he was just asking. Because he could get curious about almost anything. Maybe he really did want to know what a carbohydrate was.

"Pasta, something like that," I said. "But it doesn't matter." I figured chicken would probably be okay. It wouldn't slow me down much.

"I can fix spaghetti," he said.

I turned back, surprised. "You don't have to do that. I'll do all right without it."

"No, we can save the chicken for tomorrow." He reached into the cabinet, and took out a long, flat package and a jar of sauce. "If you should eat spaghetti, I'll fix spaghetti."

I didn't move, just watched him fill a big pot with water and set it on the stove to boil. "Anything else?" he asked.

"Well, they always drink beer at the Boston Marathon," I said.

He laughed. "Wait until you qualify for Boston. I don't want to be arrested for fixing a high-carb meal for a minor. I'll drink a beer for you."

I shouldn't have mentioned the beer. That was stupid. There was no way he would let me drink a beer. But I hadn't thought that he'd fix spaghetti just because I wanted it. Maybe my dad was doing me favors because I was number one on the team. Maybe people just treat you special when you're the best at something. If so, it felt pretty good.

"Well, thanks," I said, and headed up the stairs to my room.

Upstairs I stretched out on my bed. Parents, I thought, are forever weird—always doing things you don't expect. I figure whatever parents are for, they shouldn't drive you crazy. Most of the time, mine don't. Sometimes they're as hard to deal with as any, but never like Mr. and Mrs. Wagner. Mr. Wagner just takes over, wherever he is. Mrs. Wagner is okay if her husband isn't around, but if he is she acts like she's too embarrassed to talk, even with a kid.

When I was little, my parents could never go to the school assemblies or on fieldtrips because they were always working. And now they don't go to track meets. My dad runs a surveying crew that's out of town a lot, and my mom works in the trust department of a bank downtown. Sometimes I wish they had more time, but it usually doesn't bug me.

Every once in a while, I'll spend a weekend with my parents and think they're the greatest. But they're really different from each other. At night and on weekends my mom likes to go out and my dad stays home. I go camping with my mom sometimes. Or out to a movie, the museum downtown, an art gallery. She's crazy about travel. She has been all over the United States, and has gone to Europe and Mexico a couple of times each. Sometimes my dad and I go on trips with her, but she'll go off with some women from work too.

The main place my dad takes me is to the site where he's working. He lets me look through the theodolite or hold the stake. He and I build things together, like the treehouse in the backyard and some neat two-story birdhouses. Dad builds furniture too. Our house is filled with it, and it's good. You'd never know that it came out of our basement.

There's stuff that we all do together, but we've each got our own interests. Maybe the Wagners spend too much time together. Or maybe they shouldn't be together at all. If I were their kid, I know I would've been a lot crazier than Daryl.

I heard Mom come in downstairs. That meant our high-carb dinner would be ready soon.

That night, while I swirled the spaghetti on my fork, my folks asked about the meet. I tried to describe it without sounding too cocky.

"The best runner for Grandville's pretty good," I said. "Not great, but he's run 2:08, which isn't too bad." My dad looked up from his plate. Now he had a little bit of tomato sauce on his mustache.

"Didn't you run better than that last week?"

"Well, yeah," I said, "but that was my best ever. I don't know if I can do it again."

"You train pretty hard this week?" he asked.

"Yeah, I guess."

"You'll do well." He said it like it was already decided,

like I couldn't lose. Uh-oh, I thought. They're counting on me.

"How shall we celebrate tomorrow?" my mom asked. "Shall we go out?"

I shrugged. This was becoming too big a thing. If I lost, I'd really feel like a jerk. "Maybe we could have chicken or something," I said, remembering the uncooked food that Dad had put in the refrigerator. I lifted a huge ball of spaghetti to my mouth. Just as it got near my lips, it slid off my fork and splattered back onto the plate. Nobody said anything. Maybe my folks didn't see it. I hoped not. Here they were, talking like I could beat anyone on the track and I couldn't even get spaghetti into my mouth.

CHAPTER FIVE

The whole team took a bus to track meets at other schools, and usually it was a real zoo. We'd cruise down the interstate with guys screaming and hollering so loud I thought the windows would break. Sometimes guys tried to toss cherry bombs out the windows, but if the coaches caught you doing that, they'd pull you out of the meet. Robbie Bester always sat in the long backseat so that if a carload of girls got behind us, he could moon them.

I didn't feel like screwing around. I kept trying to remember everything Mr. Wagner had told me. Daryl sat next to me. Coach had asked him if he wanted to come along. At first he'd said no, that he and Cathy were supposed to do something that afternoon. I couldn't believe it. For months this guy had lived for track and now he was too busy? "Why aren't you coming?" I asked him. "Everybody's expecting you."

He shrugged and looked away. "I've got some studying to do, that's all."

"Forget it. You're coming," I said. "You're my good-luck charm." That was supposed to be a joke but he took it seriously.

His face got all stiff and he wouldn't look me in the eye. "Hey, what more can I do? I'm off the team! I gave you my old man. Isn't that enough?" Then he paused a second and his whole body looked like it deflated a little. He let out a breath and his shoulders slumped forward. "Never mind," he said. "I'll come."

When the bus left the school, everyone was psyched—laughing, shouting, singing. Daryl too. He laughed the way he always had when the whole team got together, like he was with his buddies. Which he was.

There was a special chant for bus trips. One guy would yell, "We're gonna kick their butts," and everyone would join in, "Yeah, we are!" Then someone else would add, "We're gonna show 'em how," and everyone would answer, "Yeah, we are!" But as we went along, I realized Daryl wasn't joining in. Once he said, "Yeah, you are," but it wasn't loud. He stared out the window as if he'd rather be somewhere else. I elbowed him, tried to talk, but he just stared out the window. I remembered his comment, "I gave you my dad." But I didn't want his dad—not nearly as much as I wanted Daryl to be the same as he had been.

His dad came on his own. Not many parents made it to the away meets but we all knew Mr. Wagner would. He never missed anything involving the track or football teams. Practice, scrimmages, every meet and game. He ran a real-estate company that had his name on it—the Wagner Company—and I guess he could leave whenever he wanted to. During the season, he may have put more time into our teams than into his own business. I'll bet there were even weeks I saw him more than Mrs. Wagner did.

When we got off the bus, I looked for him first thing. Until I found him, I felt kind of nervous. Because, really, Daryl wasn't my only good-luck charm. His dad was too. As soon as I saw him, I felt stronger, ready to run. Mr. Wagner could be a pain but he had confidence in me. With him there, my personal coach, I knew I could win. In a way, I really did feel like his second son, just as he'd said.

The half-mile is run late in the meets, right after the 180-yard low hurdles. But I started warming up early. I would be ready, no matter what. But first, I couldn't keep from yawning. "You're just nervous, Tiger," Mr. Wagner said, slapping me on the back. "But if you yawn in the race, you're in big trouble." He had set a goal for me of 2:04, two seconds better than I'd ever run before. I was supposed to run the first quarter-mile in 57 seconds and the second in 67. I'd agreed to it, but I wasn't sure it was possible.

While I warmed up, Daryl stood all by himself. He watched all the events, but he didn't stay with his old man the way I had expected. He even avoided the team, and when the meet started he sat by himself in the stands. When the half-mile was twenty minutes away, I started to stride about eighty yards down the infield and then back again. Mr. Wagner had told me to do that to loosen up. Daryl came down onto the field. Each time down the field I passed him, but he always seemed busy with something else.

Maybe I did too many of those strides. By the time the half-mile was called, I felt worn out, like I wouldn't have the strength even to finish, let alone win.

We lined up together, three guys from each team. I set up my block in the second lane. The other team's runners looked real puzzled by it. Their best runner was a guy named Greene, a skinny kid with curly black hair. Everyone stood at the line, leaning forward, their arms dangling. I was straddling my block.

When the starter said, "Runners get ready," I lowered to the block, my right knee touching the ground. Grandville had a good composition track. It should be fast, I thought. I wiped my hands on my butt and placed my fingers right behind the line, the way the sprinters do.

"This is yours, Carl Lewis." I looked up and to my left.

Mr. Wagner was there in the infield, beside the line, a stopwatch in his hand. He wanted me to burst out of the blocks the way Lewis did in the sprints. In Mr. Wagner's mirrored glasses, I could see the reflections of all the runners on the track.

"Get set." I rose up. In that position, you should form a straight line from your butt to your neck, tensed like a coiled spring, ready. "Go!" shouted the starter and he shot off his gun.

Well, I *thought* I was ready. But when that gun went off it seemed to take a second for the message to get through to my legs. I didn't shoot out as fast as I should have. The Grandville runner was in front of me when we hit the first turn. His shirt hung out loose and flapped in my face like a tail. Get that guy, I thought, get him.

At the end of 110, the middle of the turn, I thought maybe I was too tired to run well. I didn't feel as strong as I had in practice all that week. But I stayed right behind that flapping tail. Get him!

I tried to pass Greene on the backstretch but couldn't. He was a smart runner—he kept his elbows out like they were weapons. And he positioned himself at the outside of the first lane. I almost could have passed him on the inside, but Mr. Wagner had warned that if I tried that and made one wrong step I might end up on my face.

I stayed behind on the third and fourth turns. That's

where Daryl was standing, in the infield. He hadn't said anything to me since we had reached the track but now he was leaning out and screaming, "Go, Curt! Go!" I did, and poured it on. Just seeing Daryl there—cheering for *me*—was all the encouragement I needed. His dad was at the finish line. He didn't yell like everybody around him, just kept his eyes on the watch. All business. I knew I should have been in the lead long ago. But maybe I could still make it up. We had another lap to go.

I stretched out my stride so it was almost as fast as my kick. Near the line, I drew even with Greene. I heard Mr. Wagner say "58" and I was past him. Just a second slower than we'd planned! I could still win. If I could run 66 seconds on the second lap I'd still hit 2:04.

I edged in front of Greene and leaned into the curve. He felt so close behind me I thought he might step on my heels. I sped up some, just to protect myself. I wondered who this guy was. Did he have a super kick or none at all? Coach had said his best was 2:08, but he seemed to be running a lot faster than that.

My breath came in short bursts. I filled my cheeks, blew them out, filled them again. There was no one in front of me, but Greene could still pass me on the backstretch. He was breathing hard too.

The backstretch was quiet, just our shoes digging up the track. Everyone was across the way at the finish line. And then I couldn't even hear Greene. Everything was silent, as if I were running at the beach or something. My hair beat against my neck, pushing me along even faster.

Sweat fell into my eyes. I blinked them a couple of times and leaned into the third and fourth turns. Daryl was still there, clapping. He ran along as I approached him, waving me on. "You got him, you got him," he shouted. He was getting hoarse. For a second I wondered if he would push his heart too much, but then I was past him, past the spot where he had fallen. All I could see was the tape in front of me. Eighty yards to go.

Everyone was screaming. I didn't know if that was because I was winning or because Greene was getting ready to pass me. I didn't hear him but I wasn't listening too closely either. I leaned a little more, my gut was aching, and then I was beyond the finish line. I must have broken the tape but I hadn't even noticed it.

As I passed him, Mr. Wagner shouted out, "2:04, 2:05." Almost our goal! Another personal best! I slowed down and glanced back to my right. Greene was almost ten yards behind. I'd won easily.

By the time I stopped, Daryl had run up and jumped on me, almost knocking me down. He was making whooping noises as if it were even more exciting than if he'd won. We hugged right there on the track. I grabbed his hand, raised it over our heads, and we ran around the turn. It wasn't exactly a victory lap, that would have been hotdogging it, but I couldn't just stop. He tried to let go, but I held on and took him around with me, maybe fifty yards.

This one was for Daryl, I said to myself, my best friend. It was the first race I'd ever won. Five points for the team. I could feel him try to take his hand down but I wouldn't let him. I squeezed it tight and ran a few more yards. "Oh man, that was great," Daryl shouted. He said it for both of us.

CHAPTER SIX

My first win ever! It was celebration time! I wanted fireworks, newspaper headlines, a feast! My mom would probably plan something special for that night, but I hoped it would be something more than that dumb chicken I had suggested. Mexican food is my favorite. Maybe we could go out for tacos.

But even before the meet was over, Mr. Wagner told me we were going to his house for dinner. He said Mrs. Wagner had already talked with my mom. That probably meant nothing Mexican, but it would be good, no matter what. He said they'd made arrangements that morning. "It all hinged on your winning," he explained. "Second place, and you'd have eaten cold beans by yourself." He was probably kidding about the beans. At least I think so.

The bus ride home felt like my birthday and Christmas and the last day of school all rolled into one. I couldn't stop laughing, screaming at the cars that passed. "Your trunk's on fire," I yelled at a BMW that passed us. I pointed to the rear of the car. The driver, a guy in glasses and slicked-back black hair, squinted up at me and then turned around, wondering what was wrong. We howled.

I had won something! Guys like Robbie Bester, who had barely even noticed me before, now sounded like my best friends. "You were looking good out there, Curtis, looking good," Robbie shouted across four rows of seats, his fists raised in the air. And he was right. Mr. Wagner had said my time was 2:04.2.

When we left Grandville, Daryl and I were sitting together, but after fifteen minutes he said, "Listen, I want to talk with Coach," and he moved up front. They didn't seem to be deep in conversation—I think Daryl just wanted to get away from the celebration. But what were we supposed to do? Act like we'd lost? I wondered how we could make Daryl part of the team again. You don't ask one of the best jocks in the school to carry the equipment or pick up the towels. We all knew how important sports were to him, and now they were gone. But Daryl had so many things going for him, I figured he could handle any problem he faced.

We had beaten Grandville by twenty points! Five of them were mine! Before, I had always celebrated

Daryl's wins—the passes he caught in football, the races he won, elections where he'd come out on top. And I'd enjoyed it—Daryl always let me be a part of it. But this was better than I'd ever imagined.

Everything after the race was a blur, the ride home, the locker room, the shower. If there had been rafters, I'd have swung from them. When Coach congratulated me, he said he thought I could run even faster than I already had. "Just wait," I yelled, pointing at him as if it were a challenge. "You ain't seen nothing yet." Sometimes in the past I'd felt like I didn't belong in the locker room, like I was a phony. I would try to leave as soon as I could. This time, I was one of the last ones out. My hair was wet and flew out everywhere. I'd forgotten a comb. I would've forgotten my head.

At home, when I walked in the door, my folks applauded. They had never done that before. Mr. Wagner must have called them right after the race. Mom hugged me and told me she was proud. Dad never hugs. He shook my hand. His mouth moved around so much his mustache twitched. He was trying not to break into a huge crazy smile.

"Tell us all about it, Curt, go ahead," said my mom, and they sat down to hear the story. I told them everything, about how nervous I had been, about how I wondered if I could run at all, about my time at the split, about how excited Daryl got at the end. I must have talked for ages, because I went through three glasses of pop. But my parents just sat there listening, laughing with me, being proud. We weren't like a kid and his parents who had to put up with his story. We were like friends are supposed to be, like Daryl and me. By the time I finished, we were almost late for the Wagners'. I ran up the stairs, three at a time.

In the bathroom, I tried to get my hair to lie down, but I had let it go too long after the shower. Strands stood out like spikes. To heck with it, I thought. Who cares? My mom just shook her head when she saw me. "You look like a werewolf," she laughed. Together, the three of us walked out the door and down the street. I kept talking about the race—every detail.

On the street, everything was bright green and alive with energy—the trees, bushes, grass. Most of the houses in our neighborhood have gardens out front, and flowers were everywhere. At one house, the flowers looked like they were saluting us as we walked past, a row of yellow and pink tulips at attention. I had never noticed them before, though I'd probably passed them a million times.

It was starting to get dark and the Wagners' living room had no lights on. Dad didn't knock, he just pushed open the door and shouted into the shadows, "Hello! We're here!" The music started immediately. It was a tape of the Hasely fight song. Almost no one in the school knows the words to it, but it's played at all the basketball and football games. To most of us, it's the sound of sports, lots of horns and bass drums and cymbals.

Mrs. Wagner switched on the lights. She was holding a ring of green leaves, like the laurel-leaf crowns they used to give to Olympic champions. Mr. Wagner probably made her do that, but it was still exciting. She placed the leaves on my head and kissed me on the cheek. "Congratulations, Curtis," she said, and she seemed really to mean it. The crown was too big and kept slipping over my ears. I felt silly.

Daryl was at the opposite end of the room, leaning against a door frame, his arms crossed on his chest. He was smiling but it was tight, like he had to work at it. I wondered if he was mad, and why, and at whom?

Mr. Wagner pulled me aside, wanting to go over each step of the race. He sat me down on the couch, right next to him, and started quizzing me. Why hadn't I burst out of the block the way we had practiced? Why had I let Greene stay in front on the first lap? Where did I get such a strong kick? Who was my brilliant coach who suggested the starting block?

I could have talked about the race forever. I remembered everything—where all the guys on the team had stood, what they yelled, how weak I felt after 220 yards and how strong at 660.

Now maybe this sounds like I'm making too big a deal out of one high school track meet. But, remember—I had never won anything in my life. I'd been a pretty good athlete, not the last chosen for teams but never a star. I had begun to feel like I would never be a star in anything. Not like Daryl was. For years, that had seemed all right, I guess. I was used to it. Then, all of a sudden, as the top half-miler in school, I became somebody who was noticed. It was an incredible feeling.

This seemed like the most important day of my life.

Mrs. Wagner went back to the kitchen. I could smell the chicken she was baking. She knew I loved it. I don't know why, but the chicken my dad had been cutting up at home the day before had looked gross, a dead bird with its neck in its stomach. The chicken that Mrs. Wagner fixed would be crisp, golden brown, juicy on the inside, stuffed with apples, potatoes, and garlic. She knew I could eat her chicken all week.

But as we were talking in the living room, Mr. Wagner got so intense it was embarrassing. I had had fun telling my parents about the race. But Mr. Wagner was more interested in the races still to come. "Now next week," he said, "you have to really take off at the start, and then..." I didn't want to talk about next week. I had just won *this* week! I looked around for someone to change the subject, but everyone else was talking, my dad and Daryl, Mom and Mrs. Wagner in the kitchen. I took off the crown and placed it on a table by the sofa.

Finally my dad came over and asked about an office building Mr. Wagner was fixing up. At last the subject of the conversation changed and I could slip away.

Daryl was setting the table. He hadn't said a word to me since early on the bus ride home. I excused myself and joined him.

"Hey," I said.

"Hey, yourself." He didn't even look up.

"What's up?"

"Nothing." Real abrupt, like each word would cost him money.

"Then why you acting so strange?"

He concentrated on each knife, fork, and spoon as if he were doing open-heart surgery. His forehead was wrinkled. "I'm not."

"The heck you're not."

Then he looked up like I was a total stranger, and said, "What do you care?"

"What do I care?" I kept my voice down so nobody else would hear. "Aren't we best friends? Since we were little kids? What's changed?"

Daryl stared at me a moment, then went on setting the table. Fork on the left, knife and spoon. Fork on the left, knife and spoon. When he finished, he looked up with a sheepish smile, and said, "I don't know. Things have just seemed . . . I've felt . . . weird since . . . you know. Maybe it's nothing. Come on. You want to shoot baskets or something?"

I laughed. "Sure, why not?" I knew why he'd picked that. Neither of us was great in basketball. Mr. Wagner had always wanted Daryl to go out for the team but for once Daryl refused. He never got to be better than a decent backyard player and neither was I.

Also, Daryl's parents had agreed that week that he could shoot hoops, though that was about all they had agreed on. Mrs. Wagner wanted him to do almost nothing that would even make him sweat for about three months, just to be sure he was all right. Mr. Wagner wanted him to join me on the weight training, even jog a little. He said the medicine would protect Daryl's heart, let the doctor worry about that.

There was a basket and backboard over the driveway in back. We went out and shot awhile, one on one, but we never kept score. I was a better outside shot than Daryl but he could almost always put a head fake on me and drive to the basket.

Daryl was Michael Jordan and I was Dennis Rodman. We took out a platform we'd made the summer before and each took turns jumping onto it so we could stuff the ball. As we played, I realized nothing had changed! Nothing and—I remembered the bus ride home—everything.

Mrs. Wagner called us in to dinner. She'd made a feast: besides a huge roast chicken, she had green beans, corn on the cob, tossed salad, and French bread. Daryl said there was home-made pie for dessert.

"Whoo," I told her when I was given a plate piled high. "This looks great, but I can't eat all that." She smiled, as if I'd made her day.

"Today you can," said Mr. Wagner. "Tomorrow you're back on your training."

"Tomorrow's Saturday," I reminded him.

"Your training commences at ten hundred hours, right here." I looked at Daryl, but he kept his eyes down. "From now on, you're scheduled for weight training every weekend. It did wonders for Daryl's strength and it can for you too."

"Weight training?" I looked around the room. Everyone was watching me, wondering what I would say.

"Not tomorrow," said my mom. "We have plans." I hadn't heard of any plans, but she knew I liked to sleep in on Saturdays, sometimes until almost noon.

My dad added, "We'll all be busy until at least four."

"All right, then, one hour of weight training at four thirty tomorrow. Sixteen thirty hours. Then every Saturday and Sunday morning," said Mr. Wagner. "By the conference championship we'll put some meat on your bones and power in your stride. And you can get a haircut tomorrow afternoon too."

My parents laughed. "Good luck on that," said my dad. They'd been trying to get me to cut my hair for weeks.

"Now wait a minute." I raised my hand to my hair. It was still sticking out toward all corners of the room. I'd forgotten. Mr. Wagner didn't like it even when it was combed neatly.

Daryl was staring at me. "Remember, you *can* say no." His voice was almost a whisper, but his eyes seemed to hold on to me. I thought that he wanted to say more than that.

So I looked at Mr. Wagner and said, "No."

Mr. Wagner leaned across the table. Everyone went silent. He poked his face at mine, his eyebrows pushed toward me. "You mean, no, you don't want to win?"

I looked back at him. If not for his help, I wouldn't have won today. I knew that. Without his help in the future, maybe I couldn't win again. He made me mad a lot, the way he ordered people around, but he had also made me a winner. I needed him. "I mean, no haircut," I said.

Mr. Wagner frowned, and speared a chicken leg. "We'll talk about it at sixteen thirty."

The weight training wouldn't be so bad, I thought. Whenever I had done it with Daryl, it had seemed all right. I just felt funny being bossed around. My parents would never do that.

After dinner, I figured my parents and the Wagners would talk. Well, really, Mom and Mrs. Wagner would clean up, while Dad and Mr. Wagner would go on about real estate. Daryl and I would probably go outside and mess around. Maybe shoot some more baskets. But right after dessert, Daryl said he had to leave.

"Where you going? Cathy's?"

"Kind of," he said, looking everywhere except at me. "I told her brother Danny that I'd help him build a go-cart."

"*Danny Daniels?*" That kid had *nothing* going for him. Daryl and I used to laugh about him. He was fat and awkward, a real loser. He was the kind of kid who would stay after school to clean up the science lab because he thought it was so much fun. He and Daryl had nothing in common. Nothing but Cathy, I guess. But Daryl didn't have to help Danny to make Cathy like him. She was wild about him anyway. I didn't understand. What was happening to Daryl? He grabbed his coat, muttered "I'll see you later," and was gone.

The next day I slept in and then my folks and I went out for a brunch downtown. We went to the art museum (for them) and saw a matinee movie (for me—Mom covered her eyes during the violent scenes and missed most of it). We had a great time together but I don't think it had been planned. They just wanted to stop Mr. Wagner from taking over.

But at 4:30, there I was, knocking on his door. I had been glad to get away from him for a while, but I wasn't about to turn my back on my personal coach. I looked around when Mr. Wagner opened the door. "Daryl here?" I asked.

He shook his head. "It's just us," he said. "Daryl's been gone all day. I don't know where."

I thought I knew where he was, but I didn't understand why.

CHAPTER SEVEN

Two weeks later, after dinner one night, I went into the kitchen to make a meatloaf and cheese sandwich. My dad asked if I wanted to go with him on a building project that weekend. "What's it for?" I asked.

"It's a house," he said. "A lot of churches and synagogues are working together to fix up five houses for families living in pretty awful places. Companies are donating materials and the churches get people to volunteer their labor. Chuck Bailey at work helps out every weekend. He asked if I'd come along too. How about you?"

I pulled a wedge of cheese from a plastic bag, put it on a cutting board, and began to slice it. Dad just stood there, arms crossed on his chest, waiting for me to answer. I wondered how to tell him that I really didn't want to go. I feel kind of creepy when people do that kind of do-gooder thing, as if it were their responsibility that others were poor. "Out there, buddy, it's every man for himself." Mr. Wagner had said that about running, but I could tell he meant it about everything else too. And it made sense. I didn't make those people poor. That was their problem. But I do like to work with my dad on projects and I hadn't been able to do anything with him since the season began. "I'm kind of busy this weekend," I said.

"Oh, really?" he said, looking at me closely. "What are you doing?"

"Well, I'm just busy. You know, studying, working out with the weights. I've got things to do, that's all." I put the sandwich together and took a bite. It was dry as cardboard.

While I looked in the refrigerator for the mayonnaise, Dad said, "Curt, I really wish you'd come with me."

"Are you going to make me go?" I asked when I found the jar. It was almost empty but I scraped out enough.

"Nope," he said, "I'm just asking. I think I'll ask Daryl too. He hasn't been around for a while."

"You're wasting your time," I told him. "Daryl's going to be busy. He's always busy these days." The sandwich was finally right. I picked it up with both hands.

"So are you," he said, and walked out of the room.

The bread split apart and splattered bread, cheese, meatloaf, lettuce, and tomato all over the counter. It landed, of course, mayo side down.

"All right, all right," I shouted to him. "I'll be ready at ten."

"I signed us up for eight," he said, poking his head through the kitchen doorway. "All three of us. I'll tell Daryl's dad to forget the weight lifting for one day." He paused, and looked over the pile of food that had just been a sandwich. "Thanks for coming." And he left me there to clean it up.

That Saturday, we picked up Daryl about 7:30. I didn't think he'd come. I hadn't seen much of him since the Grandville meet. But I was so busy with other things I didn't exactly cry about it. I knew that someday, maybe after track season, we'd get back together. He didn't seem to care about track anymore. He never came down to watch us practice, and he didn't come to all the meets. I could understand how it was tough to see other guys running and not be able to join them. But it wasn't just track he was avoiding. He didn't even stop to pick me up in the morning anymore. That's why I didn't expect him to come with my dad and me.

But when he got in the car, with a hammer stuck in the top of his jeans, it was just like old times. "Do I need anything else?" he asked as he got in the back.

"Nothing," said my dad. "They've got all the tools

we'll need out there. But a lot of people feel better working with their own hammer." Like him, for instance. He'd brought a whole toolbox.

"I didn't bring a saw," said Daryl, glancing my way, "'cause I figured I'd just karate chop any boards that needed cutting. That may leave some rough edges, but it'll be all right. Fact, I could give you this hammer if you want it, Curt. I'll just hammer the nails with the side of my fist."

"No, thanks," I said. "I'll spit out the nails instead. I can work a lot faster that way. That's why they call me Machine Gun Curt."

"Okay, Machine Gun," said Daryl. "Just make sure you empty your mouth before you say anything my way. I don't want no nails stuck in my cheek."

"So who would notice? Just tell Cathy it's construction-job jewelry. She'll probably want a few nails in her head too."

The whole trip out there was like that—loose, fun. It made me realize how long it had been since we'd been able to be like that together. I missed it.

The construction site was a house surrounded by old wood-frame buildings. There were people everywhere, mostly black families but a couple of groups of whites gathered across the street. Kids shouted and swung on the porches, women hung laundry in the yards, and men sat on the steps talking. None of the buildings looked good; there were missing boards, peeling paint, broken windows, and some of the roofs sank like ski slopes. Most of the things around the houses looked as broken down or patched together as the buildings. But the porches and overgrown yards were littered with toys as good as those at any house I'd seen—shiny plastic Big Wheels, robots, dolls, toy ovens, baseball mitts and bats. Maybe those people were poor, but you couldn't tell it by the stuff they got for their kids.

The people in the neighborhood seemed to be watching *us*, as if we were the day's entertainment. But except for the Carsons, the couple who lived in the house we were working on, nobody approached—not to help, not to ask questions. There seemed to be an invisible line between those of us there to work and those in the neighborhood, and nobody tried to cross it. Nobody but the Carsons. They wandered in and out of the house, their eyes wide, excited. Mr. Carson, a young guy with a scraggly beard, carried around a hammer, but mostly they told people how they wanted the place to look—the rooms, colors, furniture. Mrs. Carson pointed to the porch to show where each chair would be placed.

Their house probably had looked like those next to it once, and not that long ago. It was still unpainted, but now half the boards had been replaced with new green-dyed lumber, the kind that doesn't rot. All the glass had little stickers in the corners showing it had just been put in. Even the window frames were new, the only straight lines around. Half a dozen guys were up on the roof, hammering with a rhythm that sounded like the African drumming you hear in movies.

The friend of my dad's, Mr. Bailey, came up with a big grin on his face and his T-shirt already drenched in sweat. "About time you got here," he said to my dad, sticking out his hand to shake. "Some of us have already put in a full day's work." He greeted me and shook hands with Daryl and said that we could be the most help up on the roof. "*If* you can hammer, that is," he added.

"Are you kidding?" said Daryl immediately, grabbing for his hammer. "I was born with a hammer in my hand. I'm a steel-driving man."

"Too bad," said Mr. Bailey. "We're looking for a nail-driving man today," and he led us around back to a ladder. It was high! I looked up nervously—I could just see myself falling off and breaking my neck!—until I realized that the roof was pretty flat.

My dad went to work on something in the house, and Daryl and I climbed up to the roof behind Mr. Bailey. He introduced us to some of the guys up there. They were hammering shingles into the black paper that covered the plywood. The shingles came in two-foot sections that were shaped like three shingles each. It wasn't even 8:30 yet, and most people looked like they'd been there for a while. They hammered fast and sure, getting each nail tight in five swings, *WHAM, Wham, Wham, wham wham*, the last two smacks just to make sure the nail was in snug. Then they pulled another nail from the pouches that hung around their waists and took five more swings. When they got one section down, they pulled another from a pile beside them. It didn't look like hard work if you kept your feet braced, but they looked more sure of their efforts than we would ever be. There were even two girls there, working as fast as anybody.

Mr. Bailey led the way to a section where nobody else was working and gave each of us a pile of about twenty shingles and an apron filled with nails. My pile was only about two inches thick, but it weighed a ton. Mr. Bailey crouched down on the sloping roof, knees up by his chin, and showed us how to hammer them in, overlapping the row below by just so much, four nails across, a couple of shingles beside each other before moving up a row. He watched us each put in one shingle. Daryl took six swings on each nail and I took eight. Mr. Bailey said we were doing fine and left.

"That's all the lesson we get?" I asked.

"I guess so," said Daryl as he laid the next shingle in place. He was all attention, holding the shingle down carefully with the heel of his left hand, a nail between his fingers, and swinging the hammer high and hard. *WHAM, WHAM, Wham Wham, wham wham*, and he was on to the next nail.

I put my shingle in place, pulled out a nail, and the shingle slipped away from me. I pulled it back, placed it down, and by the time I got the nail in position, it had slipped again. Daryl was on his third shingle. *WHAM*, I swung the hammer, hit the nail on the side of its head, and it flew off toward Daryl. "If that's your machine-gun nailing, you ought to warn me," he said, not looking up.

I didn't answer and took out another nail. After three swings it was bent sideways. I pulled it out, laid it sideways on the black paper, and tried to hammer it straight. It dug into the splinters of wood. To heck with it, I thought, and picked out another. I got my first shingle in by the time Daryl was finishing his fourth. "Hey, hold on," I said. "Wait for me."

"Hold on yourself," he said, looking over at me. "This isn't a race." I wondered what he meant by that. Was he *trying* to show me up or was he just doing it without trying? For almost four hours we hammered. My back was killing me, my knees were screaming in pain, but I didn't stop. Daryl took a break after an hour, but by then he had put in about fifty shingles and I hadn't done half that many. I figured I didn't have time to stop.

By noon I was exhausted and mad as anything. Daryl hadn't said much the whole morning, and he had put in twice as many shingles as I had. My dad climbed up the ladder and poked his head over the edge. "How you guys doing?" he asked. "Great," shouted Daryl. "Look!"

It was true. *He* had done great. The shingles he had put in filled a big section of the roof while my patch was just barely coming along. I waited for him to point out how much more he had done but he never mentioned it and my dad didn't say anything.

"You guys are doing a good job," he said. "Come on, let me buy you lunch."

I wasn't sure I'd even be able to stand up but I pulled myself straight. I must have looked like an eighty-year-old cripple. "I'm gonna die," I said, trying to rub the pain out of my lower back. My thighs were so tight they didn't feel like they'd ever loosen up. "I'll never run again," I groaned. My first step toward the peak slipped, and I started down to my knees. But before I hit, Daryl grabbed me under the arms and hoisted me up.

"What do you say?" he asked. "You want to go to that Wendy's down the road?"

I flushed red when he grabbed me. It felt like he was trying to show me up again, helping me as if I were a little kid or something. I turned to him fast and must've looked like I was going to belt him or something because he looked at me confused. "What's the matter with you?" he asked. When I didn't say anything, he backed off, stepped over the peak of the roof, and climbed down the ladder.

I kept hearing his voice in my head. "What's the matter with you, what's the matter with you?" So Daryl was a better shingler than me, I thought, what's the matter with *that*? He had always been a better everything than me. Once Mr. Wagner had said to me, "Somebody's got to win every race, and somebody's got to lose. If there are six men in a race, five of them are going to lose. And they're called losers. There's only one winner." I was the loser at shingling. But at least, I realized, I was now better at *something* than he was. I was a better half-miler, even if that was mostly due to his bad heart. Hey, I'd take my accomplishments any way I could get them.

I turned and walked up to the peak of the roof and looked down. One side of the roof was almost finished, the other was about half done. It was by far the best roof in sight. The Carsons were down by the street, talking to a TV reporter, laughing as if they had just won the lottery.

The neighborhood was filled with broken-down cars and rusty shopping carts. Broken glass sparkled in the sunlight. This roof, this house, I thought, was the best built thing around. And we were part of it. Daryl and me, and the others on the roof. Together. When you do something like that, I thought to myself, why do you have to think of some people winning and some people losing, the way Mr. Wagner had said? When you work together, why do you have to have losers? The people in the neighborhood, especially the Carsons, weren't losers—they were getting a great house. And the people working on the house weren't losers either. They were doing the best job they could. And why was I so mad at Daryl for doing something well?

We talked Dad into going to Wendy's. That's not a big deal to him; he eats at burger places every day because he's always out in the field, but we don't get to go nearly often enough. Daryl and I filled up our trays—I got a double with fries, he got a chicken sandwich. (He hadn't eaten a burger since the heart attack.) My dad had a salad, if you can believe that. He eats salads a lot but it doesn't keep him from being fat. Sometimes I get scared that when I get older I'll look just like he does.

While we ate, Dad told these stories about when he first started working on houses when he was a kid. I almost left the table. First, I've heard the stories a million times, all those things about how he grew up poor—poorer, he said, than the people in the neighborhood we'd just been in. He told us how he had to go to work when he was just a kid and how the best present he ever got was a load of walnut that his dad gave him one Christmas so he could build a desk or something. Can't he come up with any new stories? Second, the way he tells the stories, they're embarrassing. He's always the fool in his own stories. It's like he's saved up every example of what an idiot he's been—every time he dropped a board on his toe or let a hammer slip from his hand or put a nail through a water pipe.

Daryl ate it up. He laughed until he was spitting out parts of his sandwich and Coke dribbled down his chin. I'd never seen him like that.

As we were leaving, he grabbed me by the arm and said, "God, your dad is incredible, those stories and all."

"What's so incredible about him?" I asked. I thought he might've been kidding.

"I mean, can you imagine my dad telling stories like that? The only thing he ever tells about growing up is how great he always was, the races he won, the tricks he played, how cool he was."

"Yeah, but maybe that's because your dad never hit himself in the head with his own hammer." That was another classic Dad story.

Daryl shook his head. "Curt, my dad screws up as much as anybody. He just never admits it. It's always somebody else's fault—Mom's, mine, some politician's. Maybe someday he'll blame you. Your dad doesn't need excuses."

I thought Daryl was missing the most important point. "Yeah, but your dad wins." I could see my dad sitting in the car, waiting for us. "In sports, business, whatever, your dad's number one. Mine's just okay in everything."

"Boy, he's really got you." Daryl saw my dad, too, and started for the car. "You two were made for each other." We waited for cars in the parking lot to pass. Then he turned toward me. "But what I don't get is that I *need* him. He may be a jerk, but he's the only dad I've got." He looked at me closely. "What's your excuse?"

I said nothing, but my head was filled with answers. He's my personal coach, I could have said. He helps me win. But Daryl knew that. I didn't have to tell him. He makes me, I could have said, more like you.

That was my best day with Daryl in a long time. When we started back on the roof, I was a lot faster than before. This time, we were almost the same speed, and it felt like we were a team. We covered the first side of the roof with shingles and then finished up on the back side. We were cruising and it felt good.

Afterward, down on the ground, all the people working on the house got together, and we opened up a cooler of drinks. That's when some of the little kids from the neighborhood came up. A few of them walked right up to us. "You gonna finish that?" one of them asked me, nodding toward my can of root beer. He was a skinny black kid, wearing just shorts, with his belly button sticking out.

"Yep," I said, and took a long pull.

"Why you want to finish that?" he asked, looking up at me with these big eyes. I couldn't believe I was having this conversation. "Because it's *mine*," I said. The kid wouldn't leave.

"Then why you working on this house?" he said. "That's my cousin's."

I shrugged. "I guess we're just being nice," I said, but that seemed kind of empty, like we were helping a sick dog or something. Nice guys, I remembered Mr. Wagner telling me, finished last. But it had felt so good helping with the house, and to be messing around with Daryl. It had felt good to be doing something for somebody else. I decided I didn't want the rest of my drink, but by then the kid was gone.

CHAPTER EIGHT

All that spring, I felt special. Even though track isn't as popular at Hasely as football or basketball, people noticed me. My name was in the newspaper. Other kids—even girls!—watched when I walked through the halls. Teachers asked me about the team. Best of all, I won every meet.

My times came down a lot, not every week, but steadily. My best time came against Weston—2:01.6. That was faster than I'd ever thought I'd be able to do. I was edging closer to two minutes. After each race, I felt I couldn't possibly go any faster. But then I lifted more weights and worked hard in practice. By the next meet, I usually cut a couple of tenths of a second off my time. And I never got beat. After five meets, I had scored twenty-one points.

Now Cathy Daniels talked to me like we were old friends. She and Daryl and I ate lunch together most days. Cathy would ask me about the team the way she used to ask Daryl. Sometimes we walked together between classes, and she wrapped both arms around her books, pressed them to her chest, and bounced her head a little. I figured, so what if she's a snob?

She played tennis a couple of times every week, getting ready for the summer tournaments. Her skin was turning deep brown, like the girls in suntan lotion ads. Also her family was one of the few in the area with a pool and she must have pulled down her bathing-suit straps, because you could see that she didn't have a line of white across her shoulders. I felt proud to be with her, even if she was really Daryl's girl.

Daryl seemed to grow quieter every week. His grades improved, though they had always been better than mine. The teachers singled him out for attention, the way the coaches had before his heart attack. We didn't have as much to talk about. We'd always had sports, but he didn't seem to care about them anymore.

One day when we were walking to school, he said, "So how's my old man doing?" I glanced over at him, but he was looking around as if he hadn't said anything strange.

"He's all right," I said. "You see him as much as I do."

"Not anymore."

I stopped, but he kept going.

"Wait a minute." I grabbed his arm. As soon as I touched him, the muscles rippled from his wrist to his shoulder. Even though I knew he couldn't be working out much, somehow he had stayed as strong as ever. Some guys claimed they'd seen him working out at the middle-school track, but he had never mentioned that. His lips were pursed tight, but he didn't say anything else. "I'm not trying to take away your old man. Why would I do that? He's helping me with track, that's all. After the season, he'll forget about me. Then you'll see him as much as ever."

Daryl shook his head. "After this season, it'll be something else. He'll push *you* to make first-string football. Or cross-country. Something. *You're* his son, now. Not his 'other' son. You're his *only* son."

"Well, what do you want me to do? Tell your dad to take a hike?"

"Fat chance." He laughed. "*Nobody* tells my dad to take a hike."

"Well, what? And why can't *we* stay friends just because I'm working out with your dad? How does that change stuff between you and me?"

We walked along in silence until Daryl said softly, without looking over at me, "Okay. You're right. It's up to me to do something, not you." We stopped at the corner. We could see the school on a little hill above the track. He nodded, eyes fixed on the distance. "It's up to me," he repeated.

"What does that mean?" I asked. He didn't answer, and then we walked on as if nothing special had been said. I knew that Daryl was so determined that if he said, "It's up to me," he must have had something specific in mind. But he wouldn't tell me what it was.

Cathy came up to me in the hall that day and asked if I knew Mariella Dickerson. I almost said, Are you kidding? *Everyone* knew Mariella Dickerson. Except for Cathy, she was probably the best-looking girl in the school—tall, with blond, curly hair that hung down to her shoulders. But she scared some guys. She was sixteen but seemed a lot older, more independent.

Her dad put on most of the rock concerts that came to town, and she met almost every rock band that passed through. Sometimes she sold tickets for the shows. Other times she got to help with the lights or the sound. She led a life that seemed different from everyone else's. Every once in a while, she even drove her parents' Miata to school. I only had my learner's permit, good for the daytime. "Yeah," I told Cathy. "I guess I know her a little."

"Well, if you wanted to get to know her a little more," she said, "I don't think she'd mind." Cathy was smiling in a way that made me think she'd been planning her words for a long time. "I know she doesn't have a date for the spring prom yet."

I almost fell over. Every guy in school would have

wanted to go out with Mariella. Just the other day she'd said hi to me in the halls. But that's all I figured she'd ever say. "Oh, yeah?" I tried to look very cool, but it was hard. "The prom? I haven't decided yet who I'm going to ask."

"Well, I guess you've decided now," she said and smiled as she walked away. I had to hold on to the wall for balance.

When I saw Mariella that afternoon I didn't know what to say. She came toward me when I was on my way to the cafeteria.

"Hi," I said as she approached.

"Oh. Hi." She seemed surprised that I'd said anything. Her hair was pulled back in a Nirvana baseball cap. She wore a purple shirt with skinny straps across her beautiful shoulders.

"How's it going?" What should I say what should I say, I wondered frantically.

"Okay." She didn't slow to talk.

"You going in to lunch?" Maybe we could complain together about the cafeteria food, I thought.

"Nope." She kept going down the hall, toward the parking lot, away. She didn't have to complain about cafeteria food. She was leaving the school to have lunch somewhere else. I wondered if Cathy had been kidding.

So I ate lunch with Daryl instead. But even that felt strange because while we were yakking, Danny

80

Daniels, creep brother of Cathy, came up. "Don't look," I said. "Guess who's here."

"Hey, Danny," said Daryl, as if his best friend had just arrived. "How you doing?"

"Hi, Daryl," and Danny sat down with us. As if we'd asked him! They started talking about the go-cart, and the best ways to get up their speed. *Their* speed. So they were a team now. Danny wasn't as fat as he had been, but he was still a loser and totally nonathletic. I mean, you can't call go-carting a sport. He had ridiculously short black hair and a pudgy round face.

"Listen, Danny," I finally said, glaring at him. "We were busy."

He didn't take the hint. "Okay. Go ahead."

"Oh, forget it." I stood up to leave. "You coming?" I said to Daryl.

He shook his head. "No, I'll stay a little longer." What a pair! The best-looking guy in the school and the biggest jerk, who looked like a blob of hairy mashed potatoes. It didn't make sense.

I couldn't figure a way to ask Mariella out. Over the next week I managed to increase our hall conversation from "Hi, how are you?" to three or four sentences, mostly about music and upcoming concerts, but there were always people around. I called her at home twice and she was never in. I got the answering machine and hung up. What message would I leave? "Mariella? This is Curt. You know, at your school? The dark-haired guy, kind of long hair? I'm on the track team? You know, in your social studies class? Yeah, that's me. Well, I was wondering . . ." *Beep!*

The prom was ten days away and I was about to give up hope. I probably shouldn't be thinking of girls anyway. That's what Mr. Wagner would have said.

Each day I was getting stronger. My clothes fit tighter. When I showered I could feel new muscles. Drying off, I checked myself out in the mirror and I looked better than I had ever expected.

"Curtis! Phone call!" My mom knocked on the bathroom door. "Want me to take a message?" I wrapped a towel around my waist and wondered if she could tell that I had been looking myself over. "It's a girl."

"No, I'm coming, I'll get it." The only time a girl ever called me was to get a homework assignment. But who was doing so badly she'd ask me?

I was still wet when I sat down on my parents' bed and picked up the phone. "Hello?" I asked tentatively.

"Curt, hi, this is Mariella. You doing all right?"

My mouth fell open. I heard a click on the line when my mom hung up downstairs. "Yeah," I said, fumbling for words. "I'm fine."

"Well, listen," she continued in the most casual voice. "I wondered if you'd like to go to the prom. If you're not already going, of course. I just wondered."

I was stunned. This couldn't be happening to me. "No, I'm not," I said. "I mean, yeah, that'd be great."

"Good, I can get my dad's car if you want. You know, the Miata. Is that okay?"

Is that okay? She said Is that okay! We talked about a half hour more, until my mom came into the room. She frowned and tapped her watch, telling me it was time to hang up.

"I gotta go," I said, scowling at my mom.

"Sure, me too. See you at school tomorrow, okay?"

"That's great," I said. But it was better than that. Lots better.

In the next couple of weeks I realized that Mariella Dickerson was even more beautiful than Cathy Daniels. Really! Because besides being great-looking, Mariella was definitely the nicest person in the world.

She got straight A's in school but she didn't act like a know-it-all. She'd met dozens of rock stars, but when their music came on the radio she didn't show off like she knew them. When she heard any kind of music, fast or slow, rock or rap or anything, she could move to it as if it were a part of her. But she didn't get freaked out when she danced with someone who was kind of awkward. With me, for instance.

At the prom I felt ridiculous in a rented tuxedo with a shirt that cut into my neck. She wore a strapless dress that somehow stayed up, I don't know how, and she was totally cool the whole night. She didn't spend hours trying to teach me how to dance the right way, like some girls would do.

She said that this summer, after the end of school, she would work every concert at the auditorium. "I can get you free tickets if you want." She was definitely too good to be true. She said she had wanted to get to know me even before track season. And I think she meant it.

Sometimes she even let me drive the Miata.

CHAPTER NINE

After Will Stewart, the next best runner in the conference was supposed to be David Gant, a black guy from Landover. Before the season, he had transferred from some school in Tennessee. We heard stories about him setting a record there, that he was being watched by some colleges. I'd never seen him run, but his times this year had been good, down around 2:02, pretty close to my best and Will Stewart's.

Hasely met Landover in our sixth meet.

Mr. Wagner had been telling me about Gant for weeks, trying to get me ready. In every race, he said I should run not just against the other guys on the track but against Gant too. That would get me psyched.

I did it. In each race, I imagined Gant so close that I had to kick harder every time to catch him at the tape.

And I always beat him. In my mind anyway. Finally I was going to face the real David Gant. It had me excited and, I admit, a little scared. Since I hadn't been number one when we ran against Will Stewart, this would be my biggest challenge.

Before the season started, every practice had been agony. I was pushing myself, trying to keep up with Daryl, trying to get in shape. Somehow all of that must have paid off because now the practices felt great. They hurt, but the pain didn't bother me. I could see the difference.

If I kept improving, I figured maybe I really could drop below two minutes this year. I could beat Will Stewart. Mr. Wagner said his Family Record could be threatened. The Family Record was 1:57.6. It had never before seemed within reach. Now I wanted it. I wanted it bad.

But what more could I do? I ran farther and faster in practice than anyone else. Sometimes I ran with the milers for endurance, sometimes with the quarter-milers for speed. I lifted weights with Mr. Wagner every weekend in the basement. And finally I'd gotten used to the blocks, so I was usually the first one out at the gun.

On Monday, the week of the Landover meet, I was stretching in the infield when Daryl came down to the track. It was the first time he'd been there since that day he kind of half-ran and half-walked a lap. He was wearing his old team practice uniform. When he came near me, I saw something else too. He had on new warm-up shoes. I could see from the stripes on the side that they were a pair of Cheetahs. They're expensive, and a lot better than mine. He'd strapped on his ankle weights too. And behind him, Danny Daniels tagged along like a fat puppy.

Was Daryl there to train or just to mess around? Had his doctors said it was okay? Had his mom? He came over to where I was sitting on the grass, didn't say a word, and started doing jumping jacks and toe touches. Danny even did a few. Not as many as Daryl and certainly not as well, but I'd never seen Danny do anything more athletic than push open the cafeteria door. He was in shorts and a T-shirt. Even though he had lost a lot of weight, his legs still stuck out of his shorts thick and ripply. At least he didn't have big breasts like a girl, the way he used to. For a year or two we had joked that he probably wore a bigger bra than his sister. Not anymore.

Pretty soon, Daryl sat down on the grass by me to stretch. Danny did too. "So how you doing?" I asked.

Daryl looked up, but he didn't smile or anything. "Pretty good. How about you?"

"I'm all right." It was like we'd just bumped into each other on the street, like we were strangers. "You going to try to run?"

"I guess." Danny giggled at that.

"Your folks know?"

"Well..." Daryl wrinkled his forehead and looked up at me like he was seeing me for the first time. "Don't tell them, okay? My doctor pretty much said it would be all right as long as I take the medicine, he said I could exercise, but I still don't want them to find out. My mom would probably flip out, you know. And my dad..."

I nodded. If his doctor said okay, I figured he'd be fine. It seemed like a long time since that first meet. I knew his parents had been arguing about when he could exercise and how much he could do. One night Daryl and I had been watching TV at his house but listening to his parents scream at each other in the next room. Mrs. Wagner blew up in a way I had never heard before. She slammed the door and shouted, "Don't take him from me!" Daryl frowned. "They've been doing that a lot lately," he said, and turned up the TV.

I watched Danny next to him. Daryl could stretch out both legs and bend so much he lay down on them flat, the way gymnasts do. Danny could barely touch his ankles, let alone his toes. I nodded toward Danny, and said to Daryl, "You've got a shadow."

Daryl turned to me, scowling. "Listen, Curt," he said. "Danny's my friend. Okay? My friend. So don't be such a jerk to him." And then he stood up, turned his back, and walked over to the track.

Danny struggled to his feet. "Yeah," he said in his high, almost squeaky voice. "Don't be such a jerk." I wanted to bash him. He joined Daryl, and they started to jog around the track. Daryl wasn't as fast as he used to be, but it was a respectable jog. A lot of guys on the team came up and slapped five with him as he ran along. He smiled and talked with them, Danny right beside him, puffing to keep up.

Sitting there, watching him run, I wondered if maybe *I* was jealous now. Daryl had been my best friend for so long, and now I'd been replaced by this little fatso. Well, that was Daryl's choice. I was there to run, not to whine. So I got up and took off around the track. Coach had suggested that I jog two or three laps by myself before the practice began, just to loosen up. I went out steady, not too fast, and checked myself out, head to toe. My breath came lightly. Arms felt loose. No pain in my gut, my legs were strong. In half a lap, I caught Daryl and Danny and passed them easily.

Later Coach called us together and told the guys in each event what they would be doing. Because the meet was four days away, he wanted the half-milers to run distance, ten figure eights. That was about what he said every Monday.

Usually when we ran figure eights, I managed to lap some of the other guys on the team. Daryl hadn't been to practice in a long time and I wanted him to see what I could do. Showing off, I guess.

While we were all circled around Coach, Daryl and Danny stood way at the back, listening. Coach said to us, "Turn around, you guys. Daryl Wagner's back. Give him a hand." We applauded as if he'd done something special. "Daryl says his docs have let him work out a little, so he'll be running with the half-milers again." Daryl glanced at me, then looked back to Coach. Coach paused, and said in a softer voice, "It's good to have you back, Daryl. But take it easy, okay? We don't need another scare like that last one."

Daryl nodded. "Okay, Coach."

Coach went on to tell the milers what they would be doing. He reminded us that the Landover meet was Thursday, as if we didn't already know. "So far we're number one in the conference," he said, pulling his baseball cap lower on his forehead. "Landover will be our biggest threat. If we can get past them, we'll have only two more dual meets to win before the conference championship. This will probably be our toughest meet since Georgetown. If you guys win on Friday, we could take the regular season. But that's a big if. You'll have to work for it." Then he let us go to our workouts.

The half-milers gathered together around me. Since I was number one, it was my job to start them out, the way Daryl used to do. But he gathered behind like everyone else and listened to what I said. So did Danny. Daryl was right in the middle, Danny near the back. I couldn't believe that Danny would finish even one figure eight.

"Okay, you guys, let's get to it. Ten of 'em," I shouted.

"And remember Landover when you run. Ready, set, let's go get 'em!" We all took off. At the beginning, we were all bunched together. But by the time we ran up the hill to circle the football field, we began to stretch out a little. Danny was keeping up with some of the slower freshmen, which was better than I had expected.

Our second- and third-best half-milers ran in each meet, but they weren't much, about 2:10 or worse. They stayed up with me for the first figure eight, six-tenths of a mile, and then began to fade back. But someone was right behind me. I could hear his breath and his shoes pounding along the path. I turned my head. It was Daryl. I slowed down a step so he could catch up. "How you feel?" I asked.

"I'm okay," he said.

We didn't say anything for the next two figure eights, just ran along side by side. We were way out in front. Even after not running for so long, Daryl was lots faster than everyone else. "How far you going?" I asked on the fourth lap. I was beginning to breathe hard and so was he.

"Coach said ten, didn't he?"

"Yeah. But you don't have to do that."

"Don't worry about me." He edged out in front for a second as we ran down the hill but I caught him. We kept on like that, elbow to elbow, shoulder to shoulder. I couldn't believe how fast he was for someone who had been off the team for six weeks. For someone who had almost died. He kept up with me and I was in the best shape of my life.

On the seventh lap, I began to push it. Slowly, I edged in front of him. By now I wasn't just out for a casual jog, I was really turning it on. I imagined David Gant right behind me. Which wasn't hard, since Daryl was there, ready to pass if I ever slowed down.

On each loop of the figure eights, I edged a little farther in front, but not much. The other guys on the team weren't even close. We lapped four or five of them. Danny was still last, huffing and puffing like he might not be able to finish. But he kept going.

At the start of the last figure eight, I picked it up even more but I couldn't lose Daryl. He stayed right behind. As we went up the hill at the end of the first loop, I thought that this might be the hardest I'd ever run the figure eights. My arms were churning and my stride was long. Here comes Gant, I told myself, here comes Gant. I opened it up around the back of the football field. But I could still hear Gant—really it was Daryl—on my tail.

Coming down the hill I lifted my legs even higher than before and took it in two steps. That saves a little energy and lets the hill work for you. I kicked with 110 to go. Right where Daryl had collapsed against George-town. I figured he'd slow down some on this last lap. But he stayed ten, at most twelve, feet behind me, and ran all the way through the line as if it were a real meet. I was whipped. But I beat him. He must have been tired too, but he didn't look it. I slapped my arm across his shoulder. At least he was soaking wet. He'd had to work. His brown hair was matted with sweat. "That was some run," I said. "You must've been working out."

"A little," he said, and smiled. "But not this fast." It was like old times. The two of us in the lead, giving it everything, exhausted. Only this time I was first. "But listen, Curt." Daryl gasped for breath, but not much. "Don't tell my dad I was down here. Or my mom either. They'll find out eventually. But I just wanted to find out what it would feel like."

I nodded. "So how'd it feel?"

"Great," he said, puffing out his breath. "That's the first time I've run with anyone but Danny in a long time."

"Not much competition there, eh?"

We both turned around. Danny was just passing us to start his last figure eight, more than a half-mile behind us. Daryl shouted, "Go get 'em, Danny." We both watched as he waddled past. Daryl lowered his voice. "Six months ago he couldn't even do a lap. Now he's lost thirty pounds and he can run six miles."

Thirty pounds! That was about a fifth of my total weight.

We had walked to the first turn by then. I had to go. Coach always wanted us to jog a full lap after practice to stay loose. And I had to be ready for Mr. Wagner.

"Your doctors really said you could run?" I asked.

"I feel fine," he said. "I have since the day after . . . after . . . you know. With the medicine, what's to worry about?" He stepped into the infield. "I wish people would stop acting like I'm a cripple or something."

I kept on around the track. By the time I finished my lap, Danny was through with his figure eights. He was last, of course, but at least he had finished them all. Daryl went over and joined him. They walked a little ways and then headed straight for the locker room together, laughing about some joke I couldn't hear. I noticed then that Daryl still had on his ankle weights. They were wrapped thick over the tops of his new shoes, probably about two-and-a-half pounds each. I wondered how fast he could have run without them.

CHAPTER TEN

Daryl and his chubby chum came to practice together all that week. Danny plodded around the track in last place, but he finished every workout. Daryl sometimes ran with his ankle weights and sometimes without them, but I always beat him. Never by much, but I won. Then Daryl left about ten minutes before his dad got there.

The Landover meet would be at our track. That meant people would be cheering for me. Lots of people. Mariella would be there. But my parents still couldn't come.

Mom fixed lasagne the night before the meet, and my dad even gave me a sip of one of his beers. "Might as well make it a real Boston Marathon meal," he said when Mom was in the kitchen, getting ready. I took a big gulp and said, "Hey, that's not bad. What kind is this?" Like I'd been drinking beer for years. But really I thought, What's the big deal? It was bitter, and I knew that too much of it could give you a belly like my old man's. No thanks.

"Sorry I'll be out of town tomorrow," he said during dinner.

I didn't even stop scarfing up the pasta. "That's okay." I hadn't expected him to come.

"But I'll make the conference for sure," he said, almost eagerly.

I looked up, surprised. "You will?"

He nodded. "Absolutely. Wouldn't miss it."

"Both of us," added Mom. She passed me more bread, but I couldn't eat any more. The conference championship would be at Georgetown. They'd have to drive an hour to get there. I couldn't believe they'd do that. But at least they would see me run for the first time.

Thursday, the day of the Landover meet, I couldn't do any work in school. I got called on in both algebra and geography, but I never even heard the questions. All I could think about was the race. I'd have to get the lead right away, do a fast first quarter, and then pull away. Everybody on the team was psyched. In the halls between classes we gave each other high fives as we passed. We didn't have to say anything, just *slap!* and walk on by. We knew what we had to do.

My last class was a study hall in the cafeteria, and a bunch of us got together around a table in the back and talked about the meet. We had made graphs, showing the stats for everybody on both teams, for every meet. When I put my times and Gant's together, the two lines overlapped a couple of times. That meant that some weeks I was faster than he was, other weeks he was faster than I. He'd started out the season with better times, but lately mine were ahead of his.

Robbie Bester was trying to keep us cool, telling us how we were going to destroy Landover, annihilate Landover, chew them up and spit out their bones. He got pretty gross but it was funny. Robbie wasn't so bad. I used to hate him when he acted like he and his friends were better than everyone else, but I guess he'd changed.

When the bell rang for the end of school, we were standing at the cafeteria door, waiting. Before it stopped we were down the hall. Finally we could change into our uniforms. It was time to beat Landover.

Their team arrived in a big red and black bus. As the guys came off, we stood in a line in front of it, our hands clasped behind our backs. We'd planned that in study hall as a way to shake them up. We figured we'd look like a Marine review team. But they sure didn't look intimidated. Some of their guys, probably the shot-putters, were huge, more than two hundred pounds. They must have outweighed our biggest guy by about twenty pounds.

Gant was one of the first guys off the bus. I recognized him because his picture had been in the paper. But in the paper, I had seen only his face. They never mentioned that he was a giant. At least six feet three. I'd probably take three steps to every two of his. In the race, once he came after me, he'd be gone. If he was in the lead, I'd never be able to catch him.

After they left the bus, we all got together. The shot-putters were groaning. I did too. Landover looked even better than we had expected. "Hey! What're you talking about?" shouted Robbie Bester. He grabbed me by the shoulders and shook me. "Which of you has the best time?"

"I do," I said, though he already knew the answer.

"Who's had the best times most weeks this season?"

"I do."

I smiled as I remembered.

"So who's gonna win today?"

"I am!" I yelled, and we slapped hands. It was true, darn it. I knew I should win that race, but sometimes I forgot. Robbie helped me remember. I was ready to leave David Gant behind.

For the first time since the Grandville meet, I yawned a lot before the race. But this time I knew what it meant and it didn't bug me. Who wouldn't be nervous? I didn't have to ask Mr. Wagner about it. He was there, of course, the stopwatch around his neck. A cord hung out of his pants pocket that looked like it belonged to his other stopwatch. Even though Daryl wasn't running, he still brought them both.

We went into the infield for my stridings. He stood in the middle of the field and I ran from one end to the other, about half-speed, with long steps. "Stretch it out more," he said, when I passed him the first time. Another time, he adjusted my arms a little. They were swinging to the side too much. That might save a second or two and I would probably need it.

I saw Mariella at the side of the track, wearing a pair of wraparound shades that made her look like a rock star. She was with Cathy and Daryl. Daryl hadn't been to a meet since Grandville. I nodded to them but we didn't talk. I had a job to do.

Gant loosened up near the long-jump runway. When he shook his long legs and arms, they looked like they were barely connected to his body. He was about four inches taller than me, with short-cropped hair and a real young-looking face. Except for his height, he didn't look like a senior at all. I wanted him to jog so I could see his long legs in action. But all he did was exercises, even though striding would probably help him more. Didn't he know that? His coaches must not be as good as mine, I thought.

They announced the half-mile and we all lined up. Gant was on the inside and I was in lane two. He ran out about twenty yards and came back. His stride seemed to go on forever. I clenched my fists. He wouldn't get ahead, no matter what.

As usual, I was the only one with a starting block. I got ready real slow and casual, because I knew they couldn't start without me. I stood over the blocks, then knelt and stretched out my back leg. The foot pieces were just right. I exhaled a big breath and shook my hands to get out any tension that might still be there. My hands were wet so I wiped them on my shorts.

"Get set," announced the starter. He had his arm raised, a blank gun in his hand. Over his hand and wrist hung a yellow plastic hood. But I didn't watch that. You should just watch the track ahead, the place you want to run to. And with a block, you tense your body so you'll be ready to explode out of there.

"Go," he shouted, and as the gun went off, I was gone. It was my best race start ever. I was out of the blocks and up to the turn before I even realized it. Mariella, Daryl, and Cathy were about twenty yards down, so I passed them while I was still rising up from the blocks. I could see they were yelling but I couldn't hear anything. Then we hit the turn. Somebody, I figured it was Gant, was right on my tail.

Usually, I try to sprint the first 110, relax a little at the end of the turn, and then pick it up again on the straightaway where somebody could pass me. But he was so close, I was afraid that if I slowed at all he'd land on the back of my foot and we'd both go down. So I kept full speed through the turns and then continued it down the backstretch.

I heard his feet hit the track with a sound like *chooh*. A second or two later, I heard another *chooh*. A pause and then *chooh*. He might have taken half as many strides as I did. *Chooh*. I was already breathing hard and couldn't hear his breath at all. *Chooh*. He seemed like he was just taking it easy. Playing games with me. *Chooh*.

Around the third and fourth turns, I let up a little. Not much, just so I wouldn't have to sprint the whole distance. As soon as I did, he pulled even with me. Let him, I thought. He'll have to run three or four steps farther. In the end, maybe that will be the difference.

I turned it on again as I came down the straightaway. I could see the reflection in Mr. Wagner's mirrored glasses from fifty yards away. He turned his head from me to the watch and back to me. His face was expressionless, as if I were just a machine he was checking. I passed the line as he announced "54, 55." Mariella screamed something I couldn't hear. Daryl shouted that Gant was a half-step behind, and we were into the turn.

It was too fast. I'd never run a first quarter faster than 57 and I still had another lap to go. I wouldn't have anything left for the finish. I slowed a little at the 110 mark, but Gant was right there beside me again, looming over me like a tree. His legs reached out effortlessly, eating up the track. He still didn't breathe hard. His body was skinny as a stick, without much muscle, but his legs went out forever. Lots of great distance runners are built like that.

When he got beside me I turned it on just a little, to make sure he didn't pass, and went into my full sprint again at the head of the backstretch. He fell behind me just enough so I couldn't see him. But I could hear him, could imagine his long legs unrolling.

I didn't have much left. As I crossed through the silence of the backstretch, just his *chooh, chooh,* behind me, I wondered if I'd have anything left for a kick. Then we hit the turn and the crowd started cheering again. It was my crowd, all the guys at school who'd been slapping my hand, the girls who'd suddenly noticed that I was alive. Mariella. Daryl. Mr. Wagner.

Around the turn, people were bent down almost double as they screamed. My breath was pounding like it had an amplifier. That was all I could hear, that and our shoes churning up the track. *Chooh, chooh, chooh.* A hundred yards to go and Gant still wasn't breathing hard.

This time he didn't try to pass on the turn and I gave it everything I had. My breath came even harder. My gut ached. On my right, Gant, still behind me, started to edge forward. Mr. Wagner had told me to slide over when somebody was next to me like that, so he'd have to run farther outside, but I only had enough gas to race down the final stretch, my eyes on the thin, white strip above the finish line, the mirrored glasses to the left, the stopwatch raised.

Suddenly Gant began to puff and blow, puff and blow hard. I could see his legs flash into my vision, still a foot or two behind mine, and the string approached, and for the first time ever I felt it. It just kissed my chest and was gone. I'd won. Mr. Wagner shouted out, "59, two minutes." I stumbled. I thought I would fall on my face and the other guys would trample me, but I caught my balance, and felt an arm across my shoulders.

It was Gant, his baby face suddenly looking tortured, as if he'd been pushing all along. He was trying to talk, white spit at the sides of his mouth. Some words came out that I couldn't understand, and he was gone. He bent over, his hands on his knees. I slowed to a walk. My arms felt heavy as lead.

Daryl came running up to me from the infield. I tried to smile when I saw him and wondered if he'd knock me over. I couldn't have gotten out of the way if I had wanted to. "You did it you beat him!" he shouted in a rush and he lifted me into the air. My arms fell and I couldn't raise them. "You did it you beat him," I heard in my head, "you did it you beat him," and finally the words meant something. I remembered the time Mr. Wagner had called out.

I had broken two minutes.

Then everything was light. I saw Mariella jump up and down in the infield. Her hair bounced like a cloud. Her hands, clenched like fists, beat together. I grabbed Daryl's hand and ran forward a couple of steps. But he stopped and pulled our hands apart. He turned away for the infield. "This is yours," he said, and then I was past him.

CHAPTER ELEVEN

People swarmed around me like I was famous. They slapped me on the back, on the hands, on the butt. I was turning black and blue, and I didn't mind a bit. Robbie Bester sauntered up with a side-to-side roll as if he were on a boat. "And you wondered who would win!" he sneered, and then broke into a laugh like a cackle. I hung my head and mumbled, "Yeah, well, thanks for psyching me up." As usual, Robbie had done terribly in the pole vault that day, not even in the top three.

Mariella wasn't jumping up and down anymore, but her hands were still squeezed tight. She waved them in the air, as if she were shooing away flies. I heard some of the girls congratulate *her*. As if *she* had run the race.

She and Cathy came over while I was pulling on my sweatpants. They were so happy I forgot all about how my gut had been aching. Mariella hugged me right there in front of everybody, even though I was dripping with sweat. Excitement seemed to burst out from her like light from a bulb. And it was all directed at me.

You could see she didn't know what to say or how to say it. Her mouth opened and shut, but no sounds came out. That was pretty funny. She reminded me of a frog going after bugs. A beautiful blond frog in wraparound shades. A couple of the other guys on the team were there too, and they were all having a good time just watching her.

Then this big figure came up, looming over us like a rain cloud. It was Mr. Wagner. He stood there with his hands on his hips, and I knew the party was over. Mr. Wagner always acted like having a girlfriend would make me care less about track. He had said the same thing about Cathy when Daryl had been on the team. There was something about girls that he just didn't like.

His voice was deep when he spoke, as if he were addressing a crowd. "You could only beat that string bean by a tenth of a second?" That was his way of paying a compliment, by sounding tough.

"He's good," I said. Mr. Wagner didn't bother me as much as he used to, talking like that. I'd heard it for years and knew it didn't mean a thing. I let it go and pulled on my sweatshirt. But I could see Mariella and Cathy shifting their weight from one leg to the other. He didn't seem to have noticed them.

Mariella looked like a bucket of water had been dumped on her excitement. That made me mad. I was grateful to Mr. Wagner for the work he'd done with me, but I wanted to spend a few minutes with Mariella. With Mr. Wagner there, I knew I couldn't.

"You hear your time?" he asked.

I looked up at him steadily. If you let Mr. Wagner feel he had the upper hand, he'd run all over you. "Right around two minutes, wasn't it?" I tried to sound as if I'd run the time I expected. That way, he couldn't tell me how much better I should have run or how I should have slid over as I sprinted for the line.

"You were 1:59.7," he said. I stood up, not looking at him, and adjusted my pants at the waist. "You're still going to have to work if you expect to break the Family Record this year."

I shook my head. "I've already set *my* family's record."

He grinned, though it didn't make him look happy. "You've got two families now," he said. His sunglasses reflected my face, as if he were a robot and I was looking into a video screen. "You can't just drop out of this one. The Family Record is 1:57.6. Two seconds faster than you just did. But you've still got the conference championship coming up."

He spun around and walked away. Then he stopped and looked back. For a minute, he didn't say anything. He just scanned me with his video-screen eyes.

I could never read him. He looked like he might have been mad at me for not running faster. Or, he could have been getting excited about the next meets. "You choose dinner tonight," he said. "Any restaurant in town." He turned back for the starting line. As he did, I thought I heard him say "You did fine, son." I think that was it. Or he might have said "You're mine, now." You could never be sure what Mr. Wagner meant.

It seemed strange for him to tell me I could choose a restaurant, sounding like he *was* my father. The whole thing about being his second son sometimes got a little crazy. I *wasn't* his son and didn't want to be. He had a son. I was just his son's friend, and I was getting tired of all the games he made me play.

I chose Mexican, of course. Hot Mexican food covered with the hottest sauce. I love that taste, like eating lava. Not everyone can do it.

Our two families went to Pedro's Place downtown. Every table has a big basket of tortilla chips and two bowls of sauce on it. The green one is the hottest, and I dipped into it as soon as we sat down. It hit my tongue like an explosion and I knew I had chosen right.

After we gave our orders, Mr. Wagner said to my dad,

"At the beginning of this season, I would never have believed that Curt here could run 2:05, let alone break two minutes. He ran a heck of a race today. You ought to be proud of him." That was typical. He would never have told that to me but he would tell my dad.

Dad put his arm on my shoulder. "I *am* proud of him." He smiled widely, showing all his teeth, and all his chins. "Curtis knows that."

I nodded. Every night he asked me about the team, about my times and training. He had never done any of it himself, he was just excited for me. Even though he couldn't come to any of the meets, I figured my dad supported me as much as Mr. Wagner did. In his own way.

The price for Mr. Wagner's support could be high. Sometimes at night I dreamed that I fell in a race, like Jim Ryun did in the Mexico City Olympics in '68, or Mary Decker in L.A. Mr. Wagner was right there at the side of the track as I rolled over and over. Cinders cut into my skin. The track was stained red with my blood. Mr. Wagner's face got big as a tree. His mouth opened like he was going to roar something at me, but I always woke up before his words came out. I never dreamed about my parents like that.

I sat on one side of Daryl with Mr. Wagner on the other. When we all got our drinks, Mr. Wagner raised his beer mug for a toast. "For Curt," he said. "Who we all consider our son. He's already got the half-mile record for one of the families that's sitting here. Now he has to go after the record for his other family. It'll be a lot harder than your first family record." He stared steadily at me, as if it were a challenge, as he dropped his voice. "But I'll help you break it."

He reached past Daryl to click his mug against my glass and then he drank. He didn't touch his glass to anyone else's. Daryl put his glass down, as if he wouldn't join in, but Mrs. Wagner said "Daryl?" and he finally raised his glass to hers.

I wished that Daryl and I could have left the table, left the grown-ups to themselves. This whole spring had gotten ridiculously complicated and it was all because of Mr. Wagner. If he hadn't been around, Daryl wouldn't be having such a hard time about not being on the team. Without Mr. Wagner, Daryl might not have run so fast in the Georgetown race. First Mr. Wagner pushed him constantly, and then he ignored him. And he didn't ignore him because of me. I knew that. If he hadn't given all his attention to me, it would have been somebody—or something—else. But at the table Daryl looked as if he was turning into his mother, pulling his head down into his shoulders, retreating into his shell.

Sitting across from us, Mrs. Wagner tried to talk with Daryl about school, about their coming vacation. They were taking a trip that summer to look over colleges even though Daryl still had three more years of high school. His dad had said that Daryl should go to Harvard. Maybe Yale. Daryl wouldn't open his mouth. Mrs. Wagner said, "Would you like to visit any other schools in the Boston area?" Daryl just shook his head. My mom said, "Oh, I've heard such good things about Boston College." My mom was just trying to be nice. She had always liked Daryl a lot.

Mr. Wagner didn't pay her any attention, even when she talked about Harvard. "What you always used to do," he said to me, "was let up too much at the turns, as if you could relax then. I told you not to, but you still did it. But today, you couldn't get away with that. You needed a hundred percent, and you gave it. You can still cut your time a lot, but now you see the way you *should* run. We just need to polish the fine points."

I wanted to eat. The smell of my chicken enchiladas rose up around my head. The sauce was so hot that I broke into a sweat from the steam. While Mr. Wagner talked, I said "Yeah" and "Uh-huh." Sometimes, if you just respond—no matter what you say—grown-ups will think you're listening.

But it was awkward. Mr. Wagner had to lean over Daryl to talk to me. Daryl sat back in his seat so his dad wouldn't have to stretch so much. I could tell he was mad. I would have been too. Daryl could hardly eat. His dad was almost lying in his plate.

Finally I got what I thought was a great idea. It would bring Daryl into the conversation, and his dad would see that he should pay more attention to his son, his real son. I went ahead with it before I had a chance to think. I should have waited.

"You know, Mr. Wagner, Daryl's running really well in practice." Daryl put down his fork and glared at me, but I blundered ahead anyway. "A lot of times he's almost beaten me, even after all the work I've been doing." I'd promised Daryl not to mention that, but I figured this was an emergency. Somehow, we had to get his dad to notice Daryl again.

The table got quiet, except for Mr. Wagner. Even with a mouthful of burrito, he tried to talk. "Different world, Curt. Different world. It's like the difference between a world-class runner and some guy who jogs around the block every weekend in tennis shoes and madras shorts. They're both running, but with different goals. I'm not saying you're world class, but you're the conference champion if you want."

"Daryl?" said his mother. She sounded even more anxious than usual. "Are you running now?"

Daryl blushed. He looked as if he'd kill me. "Well . . ." he said slowly. "A couple of times I've jogged a little."

That's when I really screwed up. I didn't care about Mrs. Wagner. But I was afraid that Mr. Wagner wouldn't understand. If he knew how fast Daryl still was, even though he wasn't on the team, even if he didn't run in the meets, I thought he'd treat him differently. He'd be proud of him again. So I said, "Jogged a little? We ran six quarter-miles last Tuesday, and I only beat him by about a step each time. And he was wearing his ankle weights!"

"You never were a sprinter," Mr. Wagner said to me.

"Daryl?" His mother sounded upset. "Did you talk with Doctor Rosen about this?"

Daryl was moving around as if his chair was as hot as the sauce. "Well, he pretty much said I could be exercising by now."

Mrs. Wagner laughed nervously, but she didn't sound like she'd heard a joke. "But, Daryl," she insisted. "I'm sure there's a difference between just jogging a bit and joining Curtis at practice. Remember your heart."

Boy, I was sorry I'd said anything. Daryl looked at me like I was a piece of dirt. I thought I should say something to calm Mrs. Wagner, but Mr. Wagner spoke first. He waved his hand in the air.

"Don't get all upset, hon," he said. She drew back, stiff. "Daryl isn't exactly headed to the Olympics. That's too much to hope for now. His track career has been buried. It had lots of promise, but it's dead now. He'll be a scholar instead. That's just the way it goes."

He reached across the table for the medium hot sauce and spooned some onto his burrito. My mom tried to change the subject. She said something about things to see in Boston, but Mrs. Wagner wasn't listening.

Daryl wouldn't even look at me. I didn't dare say anything else. My enchilada just lay there, cooling down, a tube of food that I couldn't eat.

CHAPTER TWELVE

And I thought I'd worked hard before!

The next week Daryl pushed me even harder than David Gant had in the meet. Each workout—sprints, alternates, distances—he did all-out. So did I. But this week, I didn't win them all. Just like before his accident, he always got out faster than I did. Anything shorter than a half-mile, he came in first. I won the distances. But no matter who won, it was always close. At most just a second or two separated us.

When Daryl first beat me at practice, the other guys on the team hooted. "Hey, Curtis, you can't even beat a guy who's already been dead?" You know, tasteful comments.

But Daryl wouldn't talk with me at all. I guess he was still mad that I had told his folks he'd been working out. Or maybe he just wanted to stay mad so he'd run harder. Whatever it was, he acted like he didn't even know me.

"Daryl, stop," I puffed after one especially hard workout. "What're you trying to prove? What're you getting ready for?"

"I'm practicing, that's all," he said without even looking in my direction. "You got a problem with that?"

"I do if it's going to hurt your heart any more."

"Don't you worry about my heart. Worry about your times."

I told his dad each day how he had done. I figured he'd at least be interested and maybe he'd give Daryl some attention. He nodded as he listened, but then he used it against me. "Well I guess you better work a little harder," he said one day after I explained how well Daryl had done. After I'd already run 220 alternates for an hour in practice, he sent me out on even more.

While I ran, Mr. Wagner stood at the finish line, watching my every step. If I swung my arms out, let my head wobble, or staggered a step or two, he saw it and helped me correct it. It was a little frustrating, working so hard and still not beating Daryl consistently. But what could I do about it? I pushed myself as much as I could. Nobody, I knew, could stop Daryl from running his times.

Mr. Wagner wasn't as critical of my running as he had been. He even stopped telling me to get a haircut. I had to work more, he said, but he didn't act anymore as if I needed his help just to walk straight. That was a relief.

After practice we circled the track together. He told me stories about track stars from the time when he had run. Some of them I'd never heard of, people he had run with in high school and college. But he also talked about how excited he'd been when he heard that Roger Bannister had run the first sub-four-minute mile. That was in the spring of 1954. Mr. Wagner said he was a little younger than I am now.

"Roger Bannister." When Mr. Wagner said his name, his voice got all hushed, like he was in church. "Roger Bannister. Everyone knew that either he or an Australian named John Landy would break four minutes that spring, but we didn't know which one. Or when.

"We talked about them every day," he said. "Bannister and Landy." He didn't look at me as we walked around the backstretch and I had to hurry to catch up with him. "We placed bets on one or the other. There was a P.E. teacher at our school, an old guy who must have been at the school for about forty years. He claimed that the human body couldn't survive the pressure of that kind of speed. That a runner would die if he ran that fast. We all wanted him to be proven wrong. But to tell you the truth, we weren't really sure ourselves."

I laughed at that. People run under four minutes all

the time now. Even some guys in high school. That trainer sounded ancient, like the people who thought the world was flat. But Mr. Wagner didn't laugh. When I looked up, he had this smile on his face, as if he were a kid. I hadn't thought about Mr. Wagner ever having been young. Usually he acted like he'd been born a grown-up, like he'd never been silly or stupid.

"We used to call the paper every day to get the results of the meets in Europe. It was all we talked about. Drove my parents nuts. And when Bannister finally did it, in May sometime, it was unbelievable. Even though we'd been expecting it for more than a month. We all went wild when we heard. We felt the whole world had changed." He waved his hands excitedly as he talked. "If people could run the mile in less than four minutes," he said, "then *anything* was possible." His hands swept through the air, gesturing toward the track, to the fire station across the street, to the lake beyond it. "Anything."

"So what'd you do?" I asked.

"I ran," he said. "I went down to the school track in the middle of the night, climbed the fence, and I ran laps for . . . an hour it must have been." He put his arm on my shoulder as if we were old buddies. "I felt like I could've gone forever." His eyes stared into the distance, his lips were turned up, and Mr. Wagner actually looked happy.

Than I asked him about the time he ran the half in

1:57.6. The Family Record. At first, he refused to talk about it. It was too long ago, he said. But after I asked again, he took off with the story like he'd wanted to tell it for years. He described the race as if it had happened the week before.

"June 2, 1963," he said. "Hillside College against Western Michigan. Western had a great runner named Elmer Wattles."

"El-mer Wat-tles?" I laughed, but he just went on.

"He was a heck of a runner," Mr. Wagner insisted. By then, we had reached the locker room, but I waited for the story.

"Wattles was a short guy, no more than five-six. Built like a sprinter, with thick calves. But Western already had the best sprinters in the conference. His coach must have made him try the half instead."

He pointed at me and closed one eye, as if he were trying to make me look like someone he remembered from a long time ago. "I stood over him the way Gant towered over you last week. Soon as I saw Gant it reminded me.

"Well, in this race, the gun went off, and Wattles was gone. I never had much raw speed. Kind of like you. But I stayed close. Just a couple of steps back the first lap. Then, slowly, I poured it on. Caught him on the back-stretch of the second lap. And then I did something I tell you not to do. I stayed on the outside through the last turn. That made me run farther. But I was afraid that if I were behind when he started his kick, I'd never be able to catch him. So we hit the last stretch together and I gave it everything. More than everything. But he still outkicked me."

That surprised me. "You mean you lost?"

He nodded. "My best time ever, 1:57.6. But he ran 1:57.5. A tenth of a second, the same time you beat Gant by. It doesn't seem like much when you win. But, believe me, when you're in second place it's everything. Second place, tenth place. They're all the same. They're all losers." His lips curled as he said it, as if the thought still embarrassed him.

"You know, I think if I could do one thing over again in my life, I'd run that race. And this time, I'd give it a little more. Somehow, I'd train harder. I'd win.

"Every once in a while I still see Elmer Wattles. He lives in Bay City now. Sells siding. He's become fat and jolly, furthest thing from an athlete. Like your dad. I'll bet he hasn't run in fifteen or twenty years. I could whip him now, but who cares? I lost, Curt. I can't run that race again."

He looked down at me and took off his shades. The sun was going down but it struck his eyes and he had to squint at me, making thousands of wrinkles around his eyes. "But what I can do is show *you* how important it is to give your all. If it's a high school match, conference championship, the Olympics, whatever. If you treat it like it's the most important thing in your life, you'll never regret it."

He looked out over the football field as if he were scanning the sky for birds. For once, Mr. Wagner didn't look so cocky and know-it-all. In fact, he reminded me of those old men who sit around telling you their war stories. The kind who get mad if you ask which war.

I said, "I gotta shower, Mr. Wagner."

He jerked like I'd awakened him. "Hey! Of course! You've got a race coming up." Suddenly his voice was too loud again, like he was too sure of himself. He knew everything. Or wanted me to think he did. It was the old Mr. Wagner, the tough guy who'd never before told me he'd lost. "Get going, son. This is a big week." I turned for the locker room and left him.

I guess I'd known it was coming. On Wednesday, Coach said Daryl would run in the next meet. Coach had been watching him train, of course, and he was almost drooling at the chance to have two good half-milers on the team. He'd even talked with Daryl about it a couple of times. But he'd said he needed a note from Daryl's doctor. On Wednesday, Daryl brought it.

I never saw it. Daryl told me his doctor said the same thing he had after his heart attack: the medicine would help, it was okay to run, don't overdo it. I knew Daryl would push himself as hard as he could, that he couldn't avoid overdoing it, but I also knew he'd already been running his fastest in the last few practices. He seemed okay to me.

Thursday, the day before the Ottawa meet, Coach went through the list of guys who would be running, and he named Daryl. There was silence for a while, and then a few guys went, "Yeah!" "Back from the dead!" Some of them had nicknamed him Zombie, the Living Dead, stuff like that. Daryl didn't say anything, just nodded when Coach named him.

Coach said, "Run a good race, Daryl, but don't go out *too* fast." Everyone laughed. "All I want you to do is see how it feels. That's all." Daryl shifted his weight from foot to foot, as if he didn't want to linger on the subject. Coach said he expected me to win. I knew Ottawa didn't have anybody good. If I got pushed at all, it would come from Daryl.

When Mr. Wagner came to the track that evening, Daryl stayed. Mr. Wagner never mentioned it, but now he again had two stopwatches around his neck. He sent us out on 110 intervals. Before we started he looked over at Daryl and said, "Remember what I said this morning. Don't try too much. I want you to run comfortably."

Daryl nodded. "I know what you want." And then he beat me bad.

When the phone rang that night my mom called out,

"Curtis! It's a girl!" I assumed it was Mariella. We'd been together almost every weekend and we talked nearly every other night. My parents were hitting me with complaints about tieing up the phone too much. But it wasn't Mariella at all, it was Cathy.

"Curtis, what's this about Daryl running in the next meet?"

"Didn't he tell you?"

She sounded irritated. "No, he didn't say a word. And ever since I heard, his phone has been busy."

"Well, he says he's running."

"But why? How can he?" She was getting hysterical. "After what happened, how can he expect to . . ."

I tried to say something, but couldn't get a word in. "He's been—" "Coach said—" "His dad—"

"Oh, his dad!" she shouted, and began to cry again.

"Dinner, Curt," called my mom from downstairs.

I told Cathy I had to go.

"Can't you stop him, Curtis?" she asked. I guess she didn't know he was barely speaking to me now.

"No," I said. "I can't. But he's a big boy. He can take care of himself."

"Sure," she snapped before hanging up. "Like he took care of himself before!"

The next day, before we left for Ottawa, Mariella came up to me. She didn't say anything, just took my hand, and walked beside me. Real somber. The days were getting hot then, even at nine in the morning, but she had on a black touring jacket from one of the rock shows.

"Is it true about Daryl?" she finally asked. I said it was. She just sighed and walked along, shaking her head. "You guys," she said. It had a tone of disappointment, but also of superiority, as if Daryl and I were just kids playing stupid games. "I won't be there," she said. "I've got to work a concert tonight for my dad."

I stopped and stared at her. "You're not going to be at the meet? The Ottawa meet?" Even though Cathy didn't want Daryl to run, I knew *she* would be there.

Mariella kept on walking, leaving me behind. Over her shoulder, she said, "You think that track meet's the most important thing in the world?" I watched her walk away, down the hall. What could I do? There was no way I could make her come to the meet. No one could get Mariella to do anything she didn't want to do. That was one of the reasons I thought she was so neat. But still, I wanted her to see me!

So I used Mariella as my motivation. I'll show her, I thought to myself, I'll show her. I would run my fastest time and make her wish she had been there!

Daryl and I lined up side by side. "Good luck," I said. He didn't answer. When the gun went off I got a great start and we hit the first turn at the same time. Cathy squealed when we passed her. Daryl fell in behind me, drew even on all of the straightaways, and then dropped behind on the turns. We stayed that way through the whole first lap, and then the second lap too. I was afraid he would pass me at the end. It's hard to run in front the whole way, hitting the wind first, and I thought he might be able to save up some strength for a kick.

He did, but I kicked too. And slid over a little to the right, forcing him to the outside. When I hit the tape, I turned. Daryl was a couple of steps behind, maybe a full second. My time was 2:00.6. It was a good time, but I'd done better. And I knew Daryl could do better too.

"Good run," I said, when we'd slowed down.

He nodded, catching his breath. For a second, I wondered if he was having trouble breathing. But finally he said, "Yeah, good race." It was the first thing he'd said to me in a week. We walked together for a ways. Since the meet was at Ottawa, not many people had made the trip from our school. But Mr. Wagner came up to us, the stopwatches in his hands. "Neither one of you will win the conference with times like that," he said. Daryl just turned away, leaving his dad with me.

"You're going to have to watch out, Curt," Mr. Wagner said, nodding at Daryl with a big grin on his face. "He wants it."

CHAPTER THIRTEEN

Even though I'd won, it didn't seem like a big deal this time. I hadn't won by much and I had run faster before. I knew Daryl would do better next time. And the conference, the big race, was coming up, with Will Stewart and David Gant and, now, Daryl. I could run a good race there and still get fourth. It was a scary thought.

So when I got home and my parents wanted all the details, I didn't have much to say. "I did okay," I told them. "Not great." They didn't care. They just wanted me to do well and to them I should have been proud.

After dinner, Mom went into the breakfast room and said, "Come on over here. Let's figure out this trip." She was excited about our going to Georgia on vacation right after school was out. We had picked Georgia partially because the NCAA track championships were going to be at the University of Georgia in Athens; we could see the best college runners in the country there. That was a bonus for me, of course, but I didn't want to think about the NCAAs now. Everybody there in the half would run 1:53 or better. I couldn't even imagine going that fast. I would think about the NCAA meet only after our conference championship. I had to stay focused.

My mom waved to me. "Sit down," she said. "You haven't looked over any of these." She had been gathering brochures, maps, books, and pictures of places in Georgia that we could visit, things we should see. She had written away for literature, had searched out books at libraries and bookstores, was even rereading *Gone with the Wind*. I had told her I'd watch the movie.

She patted the chair next to her and I sat down.

"Now look at this," she said, and she pulled out the atlas and some brochures she had gotten in the mail. I knew what *she'd* want to see: museums, art galleries, stuff like that. Probably Civil War sites. My dad would want to go to some of the old cities and look at the architecture, spending all day studying molding around the doors and the way the chairs were put together. Besides the track meet, I was hot for the beaches. And I knew there was great music in Athens. REM, the Indigo Girls, and the B52s all came from there and maybe somebody great would be playing. We each had different plans for the vacation and would push and pull each other to do what we wanted. Eventually, I knew, we'd do a little bit of everything.

But thinking of music reminded me of the concert that night. "I can't, Mom," I said. "I have to meet Mariella at the show at eight o'clock. I better get going."

That wasn't exactly true, but I did want to see her.

"Then I get to plan the vacation myself," said my mom. I groaned, because if we followed her plans, we'd spend the whole time studying dead painters. "Can't we talk about it tomorrow?" I asked. "After weight training?"

"I may have it all decided by then."

I looked to my dad and made sad eyes, as if I were pleading. He nodded, which meant he would try to distract her from writing down a day-by-day schedule. Once that schedule was made we would be stuck with it. Planning the vacation was a game we had played for years. Ever since Mom planned for us to spend a whole week at some college in Chicago. That time my folks heard lectures on Impressionist art while I was stuck in a kiddy-art class working with clay and having teachers come up all the time asking what stuff meant to me "on the deepest levels." That trip convinced my dad and me that we couldn't let Mom plan our vacations all alone. Ever.

"Don't be late, Curtis," called my mom as I headed out the door. "There are great house museums in Savannah."

I walked to the concert in about twenty minutes. It would be a lot faster when I got my full license and could drive, but I still got there before the show began. Most people were already inside. I saw Mariella in the box office. Some guy was hassling her because she wouldn't sell him a ticket at a discount. I got in line behind him. She didn't notice me. "I don't care," I heard her tell him, "there are no college discounts. Never have been."

"Bull," this guy said. He was all in jeans—pants, shirt, jacket—with long greasy hair. He had to hold onto the counter for balance, as if he'd been doing something before he got there. "I got half off when Destroyer played."

"Not at this auditorium," said Mariella. "I worked that one too."

"You're lying," he shouted. "You're just trying to rip me off." His arms were waving so much he almost hit me in the chest.

"Then go talk to the cops," I said. "Come on, move on if you're not gonna get a ticket." Mariella saw me then and she looked relieved.

"Quit your pushin'," he yelled, and I thought for a second he was going to swing, but he stomped away.

"Thanks," said Mariella, and she smiled one of her knock-your-socks-off smiles, the kind that makes me stumble around like an idiot. "I'm glad you came down. How'd you do today?"

"I won," I said, and I realized I wanted to tell her all about it—about how Daryl had done, about how I was afraid he'd beat me later on, about how he looked weak right at the end. It was the kind of stuff I hadn't even thought about telling my folks. They'd be interested but they'd ask the wrong questions and maybe they'd call Daryl's parents or something. "Are you going to stay for the concert?"

"I don't know, do you want to?" she asked.

I couldn't decide. It was Tradewinds, who are good, their songs are on the radio, but they're not one of my favorites. And I couldn't talk with Mariella in there. "I don't think so."

"That's okay with me," Mariella said. I stepped aside so the others in line could buy their tickets and waited in the lobby for Mariella to finish.

She hadn't eaten yet so we shared a pizza at a place nearby. She told me about Tradewinds, how they got there late for the sound check and the drummer came up to her backstage and asked if she wanted to come up to his room for a while. She said he put his arm around her tight. "You've gotta be kidding," she said she told him, and walked away. That kind of thing happened to her a lot, guys—including seniors, or some college guys, even grown-ups—always tried to hit on her. It made me wonder what she saw in me.

After we ate, we drove around in her Miata, talking about music, and school, and my family's trip to Georgia. She knew which clubs in Athens were the best, but we weren't sure I'd be able to get in. I didn't have a fake ID and nobody would believe I was twenty-one. Then she talked again about the guy from Tradewinds. "Man, he was so gross. He was fat, and covered with sweat, and he wore one of those sleeveless T-shirts like he had a great bod to show off, though he didn't. And his breath was like old beer, you know?" She shuddered a little, as if he were right in front of her.

"Yeah, but in a way it must've been kind of neat, wasn't it?" I asked. "Having this rock star make a pass at you? I mean, I don't know what I'd do if Paula Abdul ever came up to me. You know?"

She shook her head. The top was down and her hair was blowing behind her like a scarf. "He wasn't a rock star," she said. "He was just a jerk. Just because he plays music doesn't say that much about him."

Then she reached over and put her hand on the back of my neck. "I'm glad you came tonight," she said. "I wasn't sure you would."

I leaned over and gave her a kiss, but just a quick one since the car was hitting about sixty. We knew this one place where a housing development was being built, though it wasn't ready yet. That's where we were going. It was our favorite place—quiet, isolated, no lights so you can see the stars, and nobody else seemed to know about it. She kept her arm across my shoulder. " 'Course I don't know what I would've done if that'd been Tom Cruise," she added a few minutes later. "Or Prince. Or Marky Mark. Or—"

"Enough, already!" I said. Fortunately, I knew that none of them was coming to town. And none of them knew how to be around Mariella. You didn't push her or she'd do just the opposite of what you wanted. You didn't act like you were the boss or she'd walk away. But if you just didn't think you were a big deal, if you let her know you thought she was special but not *too* special, not like she was the only person in the world, then maybe she'd think you were all right.

And none of those stars had ever been parking with Mariella before. The only problem with the Miata was the bucket seats and the stick shift in between. As we turned into the housing development, past lots with just the skeletons of houses standing, I could see the stars were out. It was a great night and I was there with a beautiful girl who somehow thought I was neat, and what else mattered?

CHAPTER FOURTEEN

Each year the last regular-season meet is always against Freeman Hills. In fact, the last game or meet in every sport is with Freeman. Our schools are supposed to be arch-enemies.

The week of the meet, we practiced like crazy. Not because of any school rivalry stuff. That's just what the sportswriters and coaches say. Since the schools are only a couple of miles apart, everybody at Hasely has friends at Freeman. We try hard, though we're not out for blood or anything, and we always win in track. Freeman has never had a strong track team.

Since the meet was scheduled for our track, we knew we'd have a good crowd. If we won, we'd finish the regular season undefeated. And then we'd run only one more time, at the conference championship one eek later. A victory would mean momentum. And a chance to show off.

Daryl and I never dogged it for a single workout. It showed. We outran everyone by a mile. Each run we ended totally wasted, and then we went out and did it again. Once Coach even yelled that we should slow down, that we were working too hard. But Mr. Wagner had said that in high school you can never train too much, so we kept it up. I won a few workouts by a step, and Daryl won the others by that same step. Cathy and Mariella even came out to the track to watch us train. That made us pour it on even more. Or it made me. I don't know about Daryl. We were friends again, but we only talked about one subject: track.

We were both pretty fanatic about our times and training, about Will Stewart and David Gant, about our school's chances of winning the conference meet. That was it. I'd never focused on anything so much in my life.

Dedication. Concentration. I'd heard people talk about those things my whole life and now I was really doing it. But instead of encouraging me, people gave me a hard time.

Teachers complained that I wasn't studying. Which was true, partly because I was working out so much. Partly because I wasn't interested. When you're winning meets, steadily lowering your time, things like Shakespeare's sonnets seem pretty ridiculous.

I didn't even spend as much time with Mariella that week as I had before. I wasn't ignoring her, but I could only concentrate on so much. Right now, it was track. I figured she could understand that. The guys in the bands her father brought to town could tell her about rehearsing for ten or twelve hours every day. It was the same thing. If you want to be good at something, no matter what it is, you have to work. And when she came to practice, she could see how well I was running, how strong I was getting. At the Freeman meet, she'd really see.

Daryl was as single-minded as I was. Maybe more. Cathy asked me once if Daryl was mad at her. I told her, "No, he's crazy about you."

"Then why doesn't he want to see me anymore?"

I tried to explain. "He does. Don't worry. There's just two more weeks left in the season. After the conference he'll be with you all the time."

"You mean running circles around a track is more important to him than I am?" She sounded offended, the way she had when she used to act so snooty.

"Right now," I told her, "you and everything else are less important than track. It's got to be that way. That's the attitude of a winner. But after the season, it'll be different. It's just a couple weeks."

She shook her head. "You guys don't know anything. You're just acting macho, that's all. I play tennis all the time with girls who are the best in the state, who win regional tournaments. Nobody acts fanatic like you're doing. Nobody!"

Well, I felt like I'd blown it again, the way I had when I talked with Daryl's parents at the Mexican restaurant. Cathy marched away like I had spit on her or something. I was just trying to tell her how it was!

Cathy's brother Danny still followed Daryl around at every practice. Lately, though, Daryl had started to ignore him too, like he had Cathy. Danny wasn't nearly as gross as he used to be. He had lost so much weight that you could see he and Cathy really did look alike. They had the same eyes and nose. When his face was under all that fat, you couldn't tell. And now Daryl, the only one who took him seriously, was leaving him behind. Danny watched him as if he wondered what he'd done wrong.

Thursday night, after practice, Mr. Wagner and I plotted my strategy for the meet. He had told Daryl earlier that he didn't want him to aim for any special time, he should run hard but not too hard. Daryl nodded but his mouth had a sour expression as he left. Just before he went up the hill to the locker room he looked back at us, sitting in the infield, and he took off at a full sprint. Mr. Wagner took out a yellow notepad. My goal this time, he said, was 1:58. I laughed.

"I'm serious, Curt. You can do it if you want."

I thought, Sure, and I could set a world record too.

But it's not real likely. The time of 1:58 was almost two seconds below what I had run against Gant. "That's a lot faster than my best," I said.

Mr. Wagner's head was bobbing even before I finished speaking. "Look at it this way," he said, and began making notes on his paper. "Don't think of it as a half-mile. Think of it as two quarters. Against Gant, you ran a 54.7 first quarter, your best ever. Make that 54 this time, faster by less than a second. You ran your second quarter in 1:05. Cut a second off that, 1:04. That adds up to 1:58."

He raised one hand and began ticking off items on his fingers. "You've had two weeks of training since you ran against Gant. Your starts are better now. All your sprint times have improved. You know you can break two minutes, so there's no psychological barrier anymore."

He went on, but I didn't hear what he was saying. The numbers 1:58, 1 minute and 58 seconds, 118 seconds, kept floating through my brain. It was fast, faster than I had ever expected to run. But I knew that I really could do it. I could. Lowering my time by 1.7 seconds seemed like an impossible task, but I knew I could cut a little less than a second off my first quarter. And it always seemed so slow to do the second quarter in 65 or worse. I ought to be able to save a second there.

"Okay." My voice sounded squeaky, like a little kid's. I cleared my throat. "Okay! I'll do it."

"You'll have to," said Mr. Wagner. He took off his shades and looked hard at me with that mean little smile of his. "You're going to have to run 1:58 just to beat Daryl."

We'd never had so many people at the track as we had for the Freeman meet. There must have been hundreds out there. At Hasely, track has never been as popular as football or basketball. But our team was so good this year that people knew about us. We had won every meet. I was psyched, ready.

Mariella had bought me a pair of wraparound shades like hers, and I wore them down to the track. As I walked from the locker room, wearing sneakers and carrying my spikes over my shoulder, people turned and noticed. Mariella came up when I reached the track. "Hey, Mr. Cool," she said. I kissed her on the lips. Right there, in front of everybody. I had just won six meets in a row, thirty points. I had broken two minutes and today I would run 1:58.

Mariella's hair was pulled back. It had bleached out a lot in the sun and looked even whiter next to her tanned face. When the season was over, we could spend the whole summer together, in town and at the lake. Everything except my trip to Georgia. Her dad was putting on a couple of music festivals outdoors at the stadium. She had promised to take me backstage.

"Good luck," she said, and squeezed my hand. "Hope

you break two again." Finally she was beginning to care about track. She was learning some of the people, the times. She would never act like it was a big deal, but I think she respected me for doing well.

I loosened up, did my stridings, checked in with Mr. Wagner. For a while I had thought about wearing the shades during the race, but that seemed too much like hotdogging it. I gave them to Mariella to hold fifteen minutes before my event.

The whole meet went well. Guys who hadn't done much all year, like Robbie Bester, suddenly won major points. Robbie placed first in the pole vault, the only time all year. No one could believe it! We were beating Freeman in almost every event. The half would be the same. It would be my turn. As I warmed up, I could feel myself getting pumped. I knew I could run 1:58 that day.

When we lined up, my blocks felt good. By now I was used to them. Mr. Wagner had given me a pile of magazines and books about running, and I'd studied all the great sprinters. I saw the way they charged out of the blocks, heads up, arms pumping, their legs reaching out. At last I had learned to copy them.

The starter raised his gun. I was poised, ready to burst out. Next to me, Daryl stood, bent slightly at the waist, fingers curled until his thumb and forefinger touched. His jaw was tensed like his dad's when he concentrated.

139

The gun exploded and I was gone. From everyone but Daryl. Even without blocks, he was a step ahead of me. I couldn't have started any better, but I was still in second. At the first turn, I settled in behind him. For a while, I thought, you can give *me* wind resistance. I never slowed, even a little, on the first turns. I was right on Daryl's heels.

As we were coming out of them, I poured it on, almost my full sprint. By the 220 mark, I drew up to Daryl and eased past him as we reached the next turns. Then he settled back behind me. I was in first. He would have to pass me, if he could.

The track was crowded with people. Usually they're just near the start and finish, but this time they stretched all the way around, all 440 yards. They were waving their hands, shouting, but I couldn't hear a word. I looked down the straightaway as I came out of the last turn and powered into a full sprint. Even though it was just the first lap. I wanted 54 seconds. I was breathing hard already. At the line, Mr. Wagner called out "54" an instant after I passed him. By the time he said "55," I was on my way to the turn. I had beaten 54 seconds, my fastest first quarter ever.

But Daryl was still on my butt. I could hear him. Out of the side of my eye, I even thought I saw him. I told myself not to look. Just by turning your head you might lose a couple tenths of a second. Daryl exploded out of the turns the way I had on the first lap. We were shoulder to shoulder on the backstretch. I sprinted as hard as I could. Daryl couldn't pass. When we hit the turns, he was still behind me.

I started my final sprint as we came out of the last turn but my legs felt heavy. I drove them as hard as I could. Daryl pulled up beside me. I leaned a little more. No pain, no gain, I thought, no pain, no gain. I powered my arms. I hurt.

There was no way I could have run faster, but Daryl steadily eased out. His chest was just beyond mine. Then he had a step on me. I heard some sound, a kind of a stretched-out groaning noise. Then I realized it was coming from me. I didn't even know I'd made it. Daryl hit the tape a half-step before me. Mr. Wagner shouted "1:58" as we passed him, then "1:59." I was almost exactly on target. The fastest time I had ever run! But Daryl still beat me.

I nearly collapsed as I came through the line. But Daryl reached back to me and put his arm around my shoulder. "Good race," he gasped. His face was flushed bright red. He was pulling for breath. He had as little energy left as I did. I could only nod.

All the guys surrounded Daryl. Mariella came up with her lips pursed, as if she didn't know what to say, and offered me the shades. "What a race," she said. I turned away. It was stupid to have worn the shades before the race. I'd made a fool of myself.

Mr. Wagner approached, a stopwatch in each hand.

He raised up the one in his left hand for me to see. I couldn't read it. Sweat dripped into my eyes. "It's 1:58.2," he said, a big smile across his face.

Yeah, I thought, but I lost.

"I told you you'd have to hit 1:58 to win."

Then Mr. Wagner walked past, left me there with Mariella, and went up to Daryl. I saw him hold out the other stopwatch in his right hand. "You ran 1:58 flat, Tiger," he said. "You may break the Family Record after all." Daryl was bent over, his head lowered. You could see he was exhausted. But he nodded, glanced up at his dad, and then looked back to the ground. "I'll get it," I heard him say. "I'll get it."

"That's the spirit," said Mr. Wagner. He patted Daryl on the butt. "That's the Wagner spirit." He beamed, and looked around for someone to boast to.

"You ran great," Mariella said to me. "Really." She didn't understand at all. She thought second place mattered.

CHAPTER FIFTEEN

Mr. Wagner invited my family over for a victory celebration, but I told him I didn't need to celebrate a loss. He understood. He was going over the race with Daryl, talking strategy. Daryl was listening, but I could see him watching his dad with one eye closed. He looked like he was thinking, "Hey! I knew I could get you back." And I was left by myself in the infield.

I felt more alone than I'd been in months. Mariella stayed nearby, but at a distance, as if she were scared she'd say or do the wrong thing. Finally, I told her that I wasn't mad, just bummed. "But what can I do to help?" she asked. Her face was squinched up like she was in as much pain as I was.

"Nothing," I said. "I just need to be alone for a while."

As she walked away, I almost called her back. She wanted so much to help me feel better. But I was the one who had screwed up.

Everywhere, people were gathered in groups: guys being congratulated by their parents or their friends. Daryl had a lot of guys from the team around him, all listening to Mr. Wagner.

Then I saw Danny, hovering a couple of yards away from Daryl. He looked like he wanted to approach but was afraid. Maybe Daryl had already told him to leave. Bad as I felt, Danny looked even worse. Like he'd just lost his best friend. I guess he had.

Danny looked so pitiful I walked up to him. He never even saw me. He was staring at Daryl as if he were watching his future disappear. When I got near, he noticed me and pulled back a step. He set his shoulders, braced for an insult, I guess. "Hey," I said. "He ran a great race, didn't he?"

Danny beamed, still wary, but I could see how excited he was. "It was incredible," he said. "I didn't think he'd beat you."

Danny looked like a kid who'd been invited into a major-league dugout to sit next to his heroes. It was kind of neat. But sad too. I mean, Daryl isn't exactly a home-run king. He's just a good high school runner.

"Well, you're running pretty good, too," I said. "A lot faster in practice than you used to." He broke out smiling again, his lips pulled way back from his teeth.

"You really think so?" he asked, as if he hadn't expected anyone to have noticed.

"Sure," I said. "Everyone knows that. Even Coach. You might even be able to run in the meets next year. I mean, if you really work between now and then."

His eyes bugged open as if I'd just offered him a million bucks. "You think I could make the team?" He sounded shocked, amazed at the thought. Uh-oh, I thought. Better not get him too excited.

"Well, you'll have to train a lot. But if you keep at it, maybe you could be the number three half-miler next year. Behind Daryl and me. Right now, the other guys are nothing." Jeez, I thought, that's a stupid way to compliment somebody. But he didn't seem offended. He whispered, "Wow. On the team."

"I'll try, Curtis," he finally said. "If you really think I could make it. I'll try awful hard. Thanks." As he walked away, he seemed to bounce along like he was on a pogo stick. His legs were still thick, but they didn't jiggle the way they used to. He could try different events until he found the right one. If he could some-how turn that fat into muscle, maybe he could become a shot-putter. When he was halfway across the track he took off running, as if he was too excited to walk.

Daryl still had his group around him. His face was set in a stiff, serious expression. He looked at his dad, who was kneeling down and writing on a piece of paper, probably explaining the way he wanted Daryl to run in the conference championship. They looked almost exactly alike. I thought to myself, they can have each other.

I remembered Mr. Wagner saying, "Winning isn't everything. But it's a lot better than anything else." That's sick, I realized, and turned away. Maybe Mariella hasn't left yet, I thought. She'd said that I ran a good race. And I did. It was my best time by more than a second. Why complain about that? I saw her heading for the parking lot. I raced across the infield to catch her.

The whole week before the Freeman race, I'd boasted to my parents about how I was going to win. I'd shown them a chart with my times, and explained what had happened in each race. I'd told them I'd scored 31 points so far out of a possible 35, and that I could end with 36 out of 40 if I won against Freeman Hills.

I had mentioned that Daryl was running well, but I guess I hadn't taken him that seriously. Sure, he beat me in practice sometimes, but I thought he'd psych himself out in a meet. So how could I tell my folks that I'd blown it?

When I walked in the door, I smelled a celebration meal. Mexican. Like my mom had just assumed I'd win. Chili was bubbling on the stove. I dropped my books on the table in the hall, and entered the kitchen. "Don't ask," I told her. "I lost."

"Oh, no," she said, looking up. "What happened?" It sounded as if she were talking with a little kid who had skinned his knee.

"I lost, that's all. I didn't run the fastest."

"Well, what was your time?" she asked. She had reached out and taken my hand, as if we were in a soap opera or something.

I told her I'd run 1:58.2.

She looked surprised. "But isn't that your best ever?"

I shrugged and looked away. "Yeah," I said. "But I still lost."

"Well, who won?"

"Daryl."

"Oh, good for him." She turned back to the counter, and began mashing up avocadoes for guacamole. She mentioned some new movie that had just come to town. Things to see on our trip to Georgia. And a letter she'd gotten from my grandma. And she said she was proud of me for running so well.

I looked up at her when she said that. She was adding the chopped onions and jalapeño peppers to the guacamole. Dad wouldn't be home for dinner until late, she said. He had been working out of town.

She was proud of me? I had been working so hard to get Mom and Dad interested in track, in what I was doing. They had said they would be proud of me whatever I did, but I had to wonder.

"Now how long do you think it will take us to get to Georgetown? An hour?"

"Georgetown?" They had said they'd come to the conference meet, but I worried that something would come up and they wouldn't be able to make it. Especially if I didn't win every week.

"For the conference meet," she said, opening a bag of chips. "Isn't it at Georgetown?"

"Sure," I said, reaching for a handful. "You're still coming?"

"Of course we are. We said we would, didn't we?"

I didn't hear much else that she said, but right then I realized something. Track hadn't been much fun lately. Oh, it'd been exciting, winning, getting my name in the paper, having people ooh and aah over me. But I'd been nervous about it too. What if Will Stewart or David Gant beat me in the championship? What if I wasn't as good as I thought I was? As good as Mr. Wagner claimed I could be? What if I wasn't a winner?

Well, I *wasn't* a winner. Not that week. I was a second-place finisher. But my mom didn't seem to care. She was babbling on about Chicago, and grandma, and a waterfall she'd just heard about in northern Georgia. And me. She had been proud of me when I'd won. She was proud of me now. If I were fat like Danny had been or a jock like Daryl, my mom and dad, and my real friends, they'd stand by me.

Mr. Wagner wouldn't. Maybe Daryl wouldn't. I wasn't completely sure that even Mariella would. But that didn't really matter so much. I could still be special even if I wasn't number one.

When my dad got home that night, he came into the house all excited. "So how'd you do, how'd you do?" he asked.

Mom and I were watching TV and finishing the last of the guacamole and chips. I was lying flat on the couch and she was in the chair next to me. It was some dumb movie, about a hundred years old, but it was funny as anything. At least I thought it was funny. Mom and I were laughing our heads off at everything that happened, so maybe it wasn't the movie. Maybe we just felt like laughing.

"Great!" I told him. "I got my best time ever."

"All right!" he shouted. "Next comes the conference, and we'll be there!"

That night, as I was getting into bed, I realized that I'd forgotten to tell him I'd lost. And he hadn't asked.

All that week, when I looked at Daryl, I saw myself from earlier in the season. He kept his fists clenched the entire week. He cut the sleeves off a shirt so he could show off his biceps and shoulders more. "Gotta win it," he said to everyone who asked about the conference championship. There were signs all through the halls. Cathy got caught up in the excitement too. She hung on his arm and giggled a lot. People asked her how Daryl would do, and she said, "Oh, he'll win. I *know* he'll win."

Everyone forgot about me. It was like I'd never won a meet. Everyone but Mariella. Now that I didn't act like track was the only thing I was interested in, we spent more time together.

And I even messed around with Danny some. He and Mariella and I got together at lunch a couple times. At practice, Daryl didn't have time for him anymore.

It turned out that Danny had an unbelievable memory about track. He must have been reading about the Olympics and world records for years because he knew everyone in the mile, the half, and longer races too: Jim Ryun, Marty Liquori, Steve Scott, Ron Clarke, Joan Benoit. He could tell you what their best times had been, when they had set them, and where. We had a ball that week, quizzing each other.

"The 1500 meters in the '80 Olympics?" Danny shouted to me when I finished a workout one day.

"Sebastian Coe," I answered between gasps. "Is that the best you've got? The '68 Olympic Trials." I glanced at him as I cooled down. "Number three in the 800 meters."

"Third!" He shouted as if I had just broken the rules. "Tom Farrell won it."

"Yeah, but I asked for third. Ron Kutchinski, Michigan."

Danny smiled like he didn't mind missing one. "You got me. You've been doing some research." I was beginning to think that Danny was all right.

Daryl now thought that kind of thing was stupid. "What happened back then doesn't matter," he said. "This week is the thing." His old man probably had told him that. Once I tried to get his dad to tell Daryl about his race with Elmer Wattles, but he refused. "Only remember your victories," Mr. Wagner said, and marched away.

But just because I was having fun didn't mean I wasn't working. I never let up a bit. I still beat Daryl when we ran a half-mile or more. Not always, but most of the time. And Daryl beat me in the shorter distances. I felt looser than I had all year. The running books all say you should be relaxed if you're going to run well, and I was. Mr. Wagner said that, too, but everything he did made me tight.

That week, Daryl stayed with me for the special workouts with his dad. One day after practice while we were waiting for Mr. Wagner to come, I told Daryl he was too tense. "You've got to relax a little," I said. "You know, track isn't everything."

He looked at me with his eyebrows pulled down, his forehead wrinkled. "That's okay for you to say. You're number two now." The way he spoke, it sounded like an insult. But I didn't let it get to me.

"Fine," I said. "You're number one. For now anyway. I still plan to win the conference."

"Don't bet on it," he said. Like it was a challenge.

"Oh, come on," I said. "You're not going to run well if you're all tensed up like that."

"I'll beat you."

"You ought to think about other things for a change. Cathy. Danny. Your folks."

He shook his head. "If I'm tense, my mom's the reason. Go talk to her. She's freaking out all the time. Doesn't want me to run. Every night we get in this big argument. She acts like I'm a cripple or something."

"Or like your heart stopped a few months ago?"

"So what?" He put his hands on his hips and stepped closer.

"Hey," I said. "Back down. I'm not out for a fight. Your mom's just worried."

He sighed and looked away. "Yeah, I know. But she worries too much." He held his hand over his eyes, shading them. "Where's my old man?"

"He'll be here soon. Want to jog a little?"

"I guess." We started out slowly, not much more than a walk. We had to save our energy for his dad.

"My folks are coming to the conference," I told him. I was trying to find something to talk about that wouldn't get him so mad.

"Good for you," he said without emotion. We ran

another 110 yards be..

now, we were running at a

refuses to come. She says she do..

happen." Daryl seemed to pick up the pace

fifty yards or so. "But if I did the things that

make *her* happy, my old man would go crazy. If I please

my dad, my mom acts like I'm killing her. It's stupid."

I nodded toward the football field. "There he is." Mr. Wagner was walking down toward us. "But your dad said you were a scholar now. Harvard and all. Why doesn't he get off your back when you bring home good grades?"

Daryl frowned and blew out a puff of air. "There's only one thing my old man cares about. You know that. Winning. Lots of other guys will go to Harvard too. But only one person can set the Family Record." As he spoke, he sped up to a full sprint. I wasn't expecting it. I thought we were just keeping loose. He raced out ahead of me, took the last turn, and finished fast. He beat me by ten yards.

From the other side of the track, applause rang out. "That's the Wagner finish," said Mr. Wagner. "Forget about Stewart and Gant, Curt. There's the man to beat."

When I joined Daryl, he looked me in the eye. "See?" he said, and turned back to join his dad.

CHAPTER SIXTEEN

I'd been getting ready for the conference championship for so long that it felt weird just to be normally
excited. I wasn't jumping out of my skin like before. I
didn't go through the halls wearing my shades and giving guys the high five. Daryl did stuff like that. But I was
still ready to show people that I could beat Daryl. Just
because I had lost one meet, people acted like I was
totally out of it. I'd show them. But I knew I didn't have
to show everybody on Monday. The only time that mattered was Friday at Georgetown Field.

My best time, 1:58.2, was the second fastest in the
conference. Daryl's 1:58 was best. Will Stewart had
done 1:58.9. In the last meet of the year, the day we ran
against Freeman Hills, Stewart broke two minutes
again but he still lost to David Gant, who ran 1:59.3. So

all four of us were under two minutes. But each of us knew that only one could win.

I felt like I had a fan club: Mariella, Mom, Dad. They all thought I would be first. But now I had the confidence that even if I didn't win, they wouldn't feel shattered, not the way Mr. Wagner would feel if Daryl lost.

All week Daryl's dad had gone over strategy with us. He gave us both the same goal, 1:57.5, a tenth of a second better than the Wagner Family Record. Daryl was supposed to run his first quarter in 53 seconds, which was about as fast as our top quarter-miler ran. Since my start wasn't as fast as Daryl's, I was supposed to run 53.5. Then we would both put everything into the second lap and hope to beat each other, Stewart, Gant, and the Family Record. It seemed like a lot, but I said I'd give it my best. Daryl was firmer. He said he'd do it. "That's the boy," said his dad. "I know you can do it. And remember. This is your last chance to set the record. Next year you'll run 800 meters. So there's no reason to hold anything back."

At school, Cathy claimed she might not even go to the meet. "Last night, I got a call from Mrs. Wagner," she said, looking around the halls to be sure Daryl wasn't nearby. "She asked me not to go. Said that maybe if both she and I stayed away, Daryl wouldn't go all out. He'd protect his heart. She said it was still slightly damaged."

I nodded. "But Mrs. Wagner doesn't want him to run.

Period. Daryl says his doctor told him it was okay. Said the medicine was working fine."

Cathy frowned. "Curtis, his heart stopped three months ago!" Her voice grew louder. I lowered mine, hoping she would do the same.

"I know that. And Daryl and Mr. Wagner know that too. They don't seem worried."

"No, they seem crazy. Why is this such a big deal to them? They're like . . . like track zombies."

She'd be there. I knew that. And she'd be cheering louder than anyone and she'd brag on Daryl more than even his dad. Except for Mrs. Wagner, everyone would be there. Cathy and Danny would drive up with Mariella. My parents would go up together. Robbie Bester said that Mr. Wagner probably would camp out on the infield the night before. "You can't be too early," he said in a deep voice like Mr. Wagner's.

On Friday the team got out of school after fourth period so we could get our stuff together and catch the bus. We met in the hall and headed to the locker room together. Behind us, the Pep Club started to play the Hasely fight song.

Though we were already psyched by the time we got to the meet, we still felt intimidated a little. The Georgetown track was unbelievably good, a blue, all-weather track, with lots of spring. It was built around the football field and there were permanent stands—

156

not bleachers—on every side. We arrived almost an hour before the meet and the stands were already filling up. There were even concession booths selling food. In Georgetown, track was taken seriously, a lot more than anywhere else.

Daryl didn't go up with the rest of the team. He and his dad drove together. Mr. Wagner asked if I wanted to go too, to get away from the craziness on the bus, but I said no. I didn't want to listen to his lecture about every step of the race. I'd heard it all week long.

But when I got off the bus and saw that track and those fans, saw Will Stewart surrounded by girls like a big-time hero, I wondered if maybe I should have gone with Mr. Wagner. He could be great for confidence.

All eight teams were there, everyone in school colors. The field of runners looked like a rainbow, but ours were definitely the coolest of all. Coach had gotten us new sweatsuits. They were cardinal red, with HASELY printed in blue in an arc across the front. This was our first chance to wear them and we kept rubbing our fingers over the letters. We warmed up together, staying in a group. We were a team. If we supported each other, we could leave with the conference championship. If we cheered for each other, we could all win.

So we gathered around the pits for the high jump and long jump. Usually the runners don't care much about the field events, but this time we screamed until we were almost hoarse. Everyone but Daryl. He stayed some distance away, stretching, striding, talking with his dad.

Even Robbie Bester did well. He would have had third place in the pole vault—in the conference!—but his trail hand hit the bar on his way down, and he ended up with fourth. He slammed his fist into the pit like he'd been working all year for this meet. Then he came up to Daryl and slapped hands with him. "It's up to you, brother," he shouted. Daryl nodded.

While the field events went on, I thought the meet was taking forever. I talked a little with Stewart and Gant. Stewart asked if Daryl was really going to run. When I said yes, he looked a little spooked. He must have been remembering the last time we ran against each other. Gant came up to me with his fists up, bouncing on the balls of his feet. He said he was ready to do to me what I'd done to him last time. His baby face was filled with this big, friendly smile. I smiled back. If anything, he looked even taller and skinnier than he had before.

Finally the field events ended, and the running went faster than I had expected. I got in all my stridings and warm-ups, but I didn't have as much time to rest between them as I wanted. My timing was off. Then I realized that Mr. Wagner had always directed my warm-ups before this. And today, Mr. Wagner was giving his full attention to Daryl. They were both so intense they looked like twins. Mr. Wagner was down on his knees as Daryl checked the laces on his shoes. He shook his fist in Daryl's face, as if he could scare him into running faster. For a moment, I wished that I had someone who would do that for me.

Then I looked up in the stands. My parents were in the third row. Mariella, Cathy, and Danny were sitting behind them. They all waved when I looked up. When my mom lifted up her hand, I could see that her fingers were crossed.

It was time. I had been lugging my blocks around for half an hour, afraid that someone would take them and I wouldn't be able to start. When the half-mile was announced, I carried them onto the track. I'd never run a staggered start before. The guy in the second lane starts way ahead of the first, the guy in the third lane even farther ahead, and so on. We had to stay in our lanes for the first 220 yards before we could all drift back to the inside lane. That was supposed to balance out the distances around the curves. Since Daryl had had the best time all season, he started in the inside lane. I was next, then Stewart, then Gant in lane four. There were eight lanes in all. High above us, the stands rose up like an amphitheater. There were hundreds of people looking down at us.

I walked out to my spot and set up the blocks. My throat was tight, but I was ready. Ahead of me, Stewart was wiping his hands on his shorts. Beyond him, Gant looked so tall he seemed to lean out forever. I glanced behind me. Daryl was shaking his hands to keep them loose. He glared at me. I nodded, trying to say, "Let's go get them," but he just scowled. He looked at me like I was just one of the guys to beat.

His face glistened with sweat. Even his legs reflected light. Then I realized why. Daryl had shaved and oiled his legs. Sprinters can gain a couple hundredths of a second by doing that. Mr. Wagner had claimed that I could run faster if I got a haircut. He'd have said *anything* to get me to cut my hair. But Daryl must have believed it. For a moment, I wondered if maybe he wanted to win more than I did. That's what Mr. Wagner would have said. And in a close race that would matter.

The starter raised the gun, held it over his head for a second, two seconds. I took off before the explosion. After two steps, the gun fired again. A false start. In the half-mile. Me! Some people in the stands laughed at that. False starts happen a lot in the sprints and hurdles, but never in the half. If I went off too fast again, I'd be disqualified. That meant I'd have to hold back a little on the next start, give up a tenth of a second maybe. I'd lose some of that burst of speed that the blocks gave me.

But I'd read about dozens of races in which guys had one false start and then powered out to win. I knew I could still do it. I could still win.

My second start was clean. Not as fast as I would

have liked, but fast enough. By the first turn, I was already gaining on Stewart in the next lane. Gant seemed way ahead.

All the way, I could hear Daryl coming up behind me. He was already puffing heavily on the first turn. By the end of the 220, when we all pulled into the inside, he had a step on me. Despite Gant's stride, he and I were about even. Stewart had drifted back a little, but he may have had the best kick of us all, so he could save himself.

I gained a little, but when we went into the turn Daryl on the inside was a half-step ahead, so I slowed up a bit to get behind him. I didn't want to be outside and run the extra distance.

Coming down the stretch of the first lap, I pulled up beside Daryl. I wanted to take the lead before the turn. I was so focused on the race I never saw Mr. Wagner. But as we passed, I heard him say "53." On target. Another fastest first quarter ever.

I sprinted like mad down the stretch, but Daryl stayed even with me and I had to drift back behind him at the turn. I could hear someone behind me, but not too close. It felt like we were leaving Stewart and Gant behind. It was Daryl and me, Daryl and Curtis, one and two. I felt strong. I could still kick.

Down the backstretch, I pulled up alongside Daryl again. If anyone was catching us, he'd have to go even farther outside. I had a half-step on Daryl at the 220 mark but then he edged out again. I wondered what I had to do to beat this guy.

Then I remembered Mr. Wagner's race against Elmer Wattles. He had stayed on the outside of the last turn. "I was afraid that if I were behind when he started his kick, I'd never be able to catch him." That's what he'd said. And that was true for me too. So I stayed outside, like Daryl's dad had done.

I could tell it shocked Daryl. He swiveled his head and glanced at me, wondering what I was doing. I was breaking all the rules his dad had taught us, but I knew that if I came out of the turn tied for the lead, I had a chance. If I were behind, it would all be over.

When Daryl saw me stay outside, he poured it on even more. He leaned down a little, and his puffing got even harder, like he was pulling out absolutely everything to be sure he won. He stayed out in front by a half-step. His lips were pulled back, baring his teeth.

We were starting down the straightaway when he staggered. I've got it, I thought, I can win! Then I heard Daryl gasp. He slowed even more. "No!" I shouted, and pulled into the infield.

Gant went past me almost at once. He must have been just a step behind. He glanced to the side, but kept it up. I spun around as fast as I could and got back to Daryl as he was falling. Stewart was next past, and then no one came for a while. The four of us had been that far ahead.

Daryl's feet hit the little curb at the edge of the track and he collapsed. He raised his hands as his body sank. His eyes were big and round, like he had just seen something he couldn't believe, and his mouth formed a perfect O. His forehead tensed in pain. He fell onto me, his arms across my back. I had to brace my legs so we both didn't hit the ground.

I lowered him to the grass. He never said a word. His body was limp. What did they do to him before, I wondered. What did they do? I made a fist and pushed his chest, the way Dr. Whitson had done in the first meet. I pressed lightly at first, not wanting to hurt him. Then I pushed harder. His eyes were closed. His face was pale, streaked with red. Should I give mouth-to-mouth? I pounded again, and looked around. Where were the doctors who had gotten there so fast before? They were way up in the stands. I could see people hurrying down toward the field, but they were so slow. So slow.

Then I felt someone yanking at Daryl. It was Mr. Wagner, the two stopwatches still dangling from his neck. "Give him to me," he shouted. "Give him to me." He put one arm across Daryl's chest and the other under him, and tried to pull Daryl to him. I could see Daryl and me in his dad's mirrored sunglasses. We looked stretched out and bent all wrong, our skin a sickly silver. My grip on Daryl tightened. "Get the hell away from him," I snarled.

Mr. Wagner looked up at me, and his grip weakened for a moment. I laid Daryl back on the grass. His breath went out, never in, in tiny, soft puffs. I felt his wrist for a pulse. I pushed on his chest again. "Whitson!" shouted Mr. Wagner. "Get over here!" He pulled Dr. Whitson toward Daryl.

"I've been pounding the way you did, but I can't feel anything," I said. Something dripped off my cheeks onto Daryl. "I've been pushing," I said, but Dr. Whitson wasn't listening. He pounded even harder than I had. He'll hurt Daryl, I thought, but I didn't try to stop him.

I looked up in the stands. My parents, Mariella, Danny, and all the rest were standing, squinting, trying to see what had happened. I wanted to go up to them. I wanted to leave but I couldn't. People ran up. Somebody screamed.

This time, the ambulance was too late.

ABOUT THE AUTHOR

Stephen Hoffius was born in Grand Rapids, Michigan, and attended Duke University. Like the boys in *Winners and Losers*, he ran the half-mile in high school. He has written for several national publications and has covered the Olympic track-and-field trials in Eugene, Oregon.

Stephen Hoffius is the Director of Publications of the South Carolina Historical Society. He lives in Charleston, with his wife and two children.